"So nice t

He let go of her hand but kept his eyes on her. "By the way, that cake was…A-mazing. A-plus-amazing."

She grinned at that. "I'm glad you liked it. So, what's involved with running the Caldwell Foundation?"

"We train and supply rescued dogs as service dogs for disabled veterans."

"Oh, that's really amazing."

"Hey, that's my word. Find one of your own."

"Incredible," she quickly amended.

"You mean, you never would have thought a rich-man type like me had a noble bone in his body?"

"I mean—" She stopped and looked at her shoes. "Yes, that's exactly what I thought, but not anymore."

He laughed and glanced around. "I have a vet coming with his service dog to show people exactly what we can do. Come over and see me when you have a minute."

"I'll try," she replied, hoping she'd stay so busy she'd forget him. She didn't want to like Alec, but something about his shyness and his wit made her want to get to know him.

Lenora Worth writes award-winning romance and romantic suspense. Three of her books finaled in the ACFW Carol Awards, and her Love Inspired Suspense novel *Body of Evidence* became a *New York Times* bestseller. Her novella in *Mistletoe Kisses* made her a *USA TODAY* bestselling author. With sixty books published and millions in print, she goes on adventures with her retired husband, Don, and enjoys reading, baking and shopping...especially shoe shopping.

Books by Lenora Worth

Love Inspired

Men of Millbrook Lake

Lakeside Hero

Texas Hearts

A Certain Hope
A Perfect Love
A Leap of Faith

Sunset Island

The Carpenter's Wife
Heart of Stone
A Tender Touch

Hometown Princess
Hometown Sweetheart
The Doctor's Family
Sweetheart Reunion
Sweetheart Bride
Bayou Sweetheart

Visit the Author Profile page at Harlequin.com for more titles.

Lakeside Hero

Lenora Worth

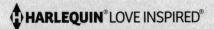

Recycling programs for this product may not exist in your area.

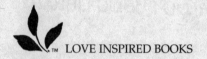 ™ LOVE INSPIRED BOOKS

ISBN-13: 978-0-373-87981-6

Lakeside Hero

Copyright © 2015 by Lenora H. Nazworth

www.Harlequin.com

Printed in U.S.A.

The water that I give them will become in them a spring which will provide them with life-giving water and give them eternal life.
—*John* 4:14

To my husband, Don,
as we celebrate forty years together.
You are my lakeside hero.

Chapter One

Alec Caldwell stared at the remains of a wedding cake.

He also took his time studying the pretty woman who'd just burst through the door with the big round platter of the leftover cake.

She had hair the color of sun on wheat, reddish and golden all at the same time. And green eyes that sparkled brighter than the fake diamonds on that fancy cake.

Alec wanted to help her but he didn't want to scare her. He'd been waiting for the valet to bring his car when the side door from what he figured to be the kitchen entrance of the Alvanetti mansion burst open and he came face-to-face with the bottom layer of the massive white wedding cake that glimmered with what looked like pearls and diamonds.

Alec had only been back in Northwest Florida for a few months now. Did they put jewelry on wedding cakes these days?

"Whoa," he said while stepping back against the warm stucco of the towering beige mansion, his hands going up to stop the woman who carried the cake in a wobbly hurry.

A face peeked around the big chunky cake. "Oh, I'm so sorry. I didn't see you—" Her eyes hit on the curving scar moving down his left jaw.

"I was about to leave," he said before she could turn away. But she didn't turn away. She just stood there, smiling across that white sea of sweetness, her expression bordering on shocked before she smoothed it into a sparkling blankness that rivaled the cake.

"Do you need help with that?" Alec asked, his manners kicking in. If he kept his face turned away into the late afternoon light maybe she wouldn't stare at his scar again.

She shook her head and laughed. "No, I'm used to this. Do you need help finding the valet?"

Offended in the highest sense, Alec frowned and then mimicked a laugh. "No. I mean, I see him coming now, but thank you."

Seriously? Had he been away at war for so long he'd forgotten how to carry on a conversation with a pretty woman? He hadn't forgotten, but he sure didn't like this feeling of being trapped. Or the way his heart seemed to skip a beat or two when she smiled.

He offered again. "While I wait, I can help you."

"I've got this," she said as she skirted around him. "Just part of the job." She motioned to a big open van. "It's going in there."

"I can see that," he replied, grinning. But he took the round platter full of cake anyway. Holding it against his chest, he took a tentative step toward the van.

Lord, don't let me fall on my face with this cake.

The woman shook her head and all that rusty hair tumbled in layers around her freckled face. "Be careful or you'll have wedding cake in your face."

"Okay." He wondered if she was as worried about his limp as he was, so he hurried ahead of her to a bright yellow-and-white van with the words *Marla's Marvelous Desserts* painted across the doors. Underneath that bold title, a depiction of luscious cakes, cupcakes, cookies and pies in all colors tempted Alec's empty stomach. In smaller black print, another proclamation: We Cater Big Events, Too!

"What do you do with leftover cake?" he asked, curiosity and hunger getting the best of him after he'd placed the partially cut cake inside the van. He hadn't eaten much at the reception and now he wasn't in such a hurry to leave after all.

She settled the cake into a waiting box and turned back to him. "What do you do with any leftovers? You eat them or share them with family or friends. Or strangers, if they ask politely."

He had to laugh at her teasing tone. "That's a nice thought."

She fluffed her hair and smiled. "I'll take this back to the shop and either cut it and wrap it up for the family or probably throw it away." She glanced back at the house. "They…don't stay around enough to eat cake and they don't care what I do with the leftovers."

"Oh, right." He understood that comment about the people who lived here. Ultrarich and always on the go. Jet-setters.

Alec had decided earlier that he'd been polite enough for one day so he'd turned away from the few stragglers still out in the garden and kept walking toward the big six-car garage of the Alvanetti estate, the slight limp in his left leg causing his steps to sound off with a now-familiar cadence. He'd driven out here on a cool April afternoon and attended this wedding in an effort to finally win over the eccentric and oh-so-rich Sonia Alvanetti. Mrs. A, as everyone called her, had agreed to write a big check for the Caldwell Foundation's Caldwell Canines Service Dog Association.

Alec would be forever grateful for that, at least.

Mrs. Alvanetti had money to spare and Alec had time to spare. So when she'd seen some flyers regarding Caldwell Canines at a recent art fair, she'd called Alec and asked him about the foundation he'd recently inherited from his deceased mother. Apparently his mother, Vivian Caldwell, had been friends with Sonia Alvanetti. Another surprise, but then, his formidable mother had always been full of surprises. Alec hated surprises, and he'd resented his unpredictable mother's eclectic friends. But this one would certainly help his cause.

Mrs. Alvanetti was in her late sixties and a tad forgetful. She'd invited him to the wedding and had insisted he should attend, but he'd had to remind her about the promised contribution to his foundation.

"Oh, silly me," she'd said with a wave of her bejeweled hand. "You know, Alec, there are a lot of eligible young ladies here."

"I'm too busy for a relationship," he'd politely told her.

Soon, she was back to asking all about Caldwell Canines and then she was off on another tangent. But she at least summoned someone who brought her a check already made out to Caldwell Canines Service Dog Association—the official title.

With a flourish, Mrs. A had put her sprawling signature on the check and smiled up at Alec. "Use this wisely, you hear?"

He'd heard, loud and clear. Mrs. Alvanetti would expect a full report.

"Mrs. A is certainly an interesting woman," he said now, grasping for some conversation.

The woman looked embarrassed. "I'm sorry. I don't normally gossip about people who employ me. I'm only here to supply the wedding cake and take back the leftovers."

"I understand," he responded, still holding the open van door. "I have to admit, I don't usually attend big functions but…it's hard to say no to Mrs. A."

The woman gave him a sympathetic stare. "She does command respect, but she's a sweet person."

Alec could agree with that. "Yes…sweet but determined and always on her way out the door to somewhere else."

Which was probably where he should be going right now.

The woman let out another wind-chimes kind of laugh. "She has a lot going on. Too many plates in the air."

Alec interpreted that to mean the lovely older lady was a bit scatterbrained, but in an I've-got-money-so-I-can-afford-to-be-eccentric kind of way.

"Yeah… I get that."

The pretty woman turned to go but then whirled back around. "I'm Marla Hamilton, by the way."

She pointed to the van. "Just in case you ever need a special dessert, say for a big party." Then she gave him a conspiring glance. "I can cut you a piece of this cake if you'd like."

"Really?" Alec grinned. "I didn't get any earlier, so how can I refuse that offer now that I've met the woman who baked it?"

"Okay, then." Grabbing a big white bag, she pulled out a plastic plate and knife and proceeded to cut a huge slab of the sugary white cake. "Here. On the house."

She layered a paper napkin over it, handed him the plate of cake, then winked and smiled up at the imposing Alvanetti house.

He shook his head, held to the van's open door like a lifeline while he accepted the cake with his other hand. "I guess I'll have a nice midnight snack later. Thank you."

Her smile brightened. "Hey, I never got your name. I mean, if you want to order cupcakes or cookies or even a wedding cake. Not that I need your name for that— not yet anyway."

Liking the way she blushed, he reached out a hand. "I'm Alec Caldwell. No wedding cake in my future, but I do love cupcakes."

She gave him a puzzled stare. "Nice to meet you, Alec Caldwell."

That halfhearted cliché didn't seem like she was really glad to meet him. Was it the scar? Or the limp? Or his name?

"You, too." He glanced at the address on the van. "So you're a local caterer?"

She went about shutting the van door. "Yes. I live right here in Millbrook. No sand or sea around but we do have Millbrook Lake and the river, of course."

He nodded. "Yeah, I kind of grew up on that lake. Love it here."

"So you're one of *the* Caldwells?"

Adjusting to her almost-condemning tone, Alec nodded. "The *only* one now."

The soft sheen of another blush colored her pretty freckles. "I'm sorry. Your mother was Vivian Caldwell?"

"Yep."

"I'm really sorry. She…uh…was one of my favorite clients."

"She was my favorite mother."

Marla's freckles grew more pronounced. And more adorable. "I'm truly sorry for your loss."

Alec smiled. "Yeah, me, too. Thanks." He changed the subject. "Millbrook is a special place. Not that far off from the coast but just far enough inland to be in another world. I got back a few months ago so I'm still trying to get into a new routine."

"I just moved back about a year ago," she said. "But you're right about Millbrook. It's home."

Nervous now, he prattled on. "It's different inland. More like farmland. Lots of ranches, horse farms and green pastures."

Her eyes held a forlorn longing. "Yes. My daddy owned some of that farmland until he retired near the other end of Millbrook Lake. My parents love the new retirement community out there."

Alec felt an instant connection that worked right along with the instant attraction. "I grew up here but left for college and didn't get back much after that. Had to come home after I got wounded and made it here a few weeks before my mother died. Retired from the marines. A captain."

Her left eyebrow lifted. "Oh, so…you're a soldier?"

"I was. Went through two deployments overseas. Retired and home for good now." He shrugged. "And trying my hand at something different."

She gave him an appreciative smile but stepped back,

her eyes going a cool green. "Okay, then. I'd better get back in there and finish cleaning up."

He bobbed his head and wondered what he'd said or done to bring about this sudden chill. "Sorry, didn't mean to hold you up."

She turned and said over her shoulder, "No problem. I think the wedding is winding down so I have to get back to the bakery and unload my things."

Alec didn't like people staring at his scar or watching him walk with this aggravating limp. And Marla Hamilton had obviously decided she didn't like him or his wounds or his name, either. For the best, he figured. She was interesting and cute but she was probably also happily married. Even if she was available, he didn't want any entanglements right now.

Calling after her, he said, "Nice meeting you, Wedding Cake Girl."

She stopped at the back door and shot him one last skeptical glance. "Nice meeting you, too, Soldier Boy."

Then she was gone about as fast as the glimmering sunset winking at him through the live oaks and palm trees.

Marla maneuvered her minivan through late afternoon traffic, her mind whirling with vivid thoughts of Soldier Boy.

Alec Caldwell. A marine. Former marine. The Alec Caldwell. Not someone who'd traveled in the same circles as she had, growing up. He was a few years older than her but she recognized the name immediately. Private schools and big boats out on the lake, lots of society events. So not her type.

But Marla was surprised that such a privileged man

had gone off to become a marine. And that he'd come back to Millbrook at all.

He fought for our country and that counts for something, she reminded herself as she turned past the old courthouse that now housed antiques and collectibles and was aptly named Courthouse Collectibles. The stately building drew tourists who bought her standing-order confections from the cute little Courthouse Café. The café was one of her regular customers, not only for the tourists but for everyone who worked and shopped in the building.

She pulled the van up to the front door of her shop, her gaze hitting on the blue Victorian storefront facade that housed her bakery on the bottom level and a two-bedroom apartment upstairs, where she lived with her preschool-aged daughter, Gabby. After parking, she sat there for a minute trying to gather her thoughts. She was almost happy again. Almost.

After she'd become a widow a year ago, she'd moved from Tallahassee back to the tiny Florida town of Millbrook. She'd needed the quietness and the quaintness of the place where she'd grown up.

And she's needed her parents nearby to help with Gabby. A daughter who had dark hair and eyes like her daddy. But Gabby would never know her daddy. Charlie Hamilton had been killed in a shootout during an armed robbery at his family's jewelry store. Gabby had witnessed most of the whole horrible scene when she and Charlie had walked in on it.

Charlie had died too young, working at a job he hated. But family had to come first. Duty had to come first. Because he felt trapped, Charlie had turned mean and angry and moody, so much so that Marla felt as if

she'd let him down in some way. The harder she tried
to please him, the worse things had become. That had
made her angry and miserable in return. They had not
been in a good place when he died.

Her husband, ever the macho thrill seeker, had
started hanging out with a lot of questionable people,
and one of them had turned on him and had planned
an elaborate robbery at the store. Charlie had walked
in after picking up Gabby at day care, had seen what
was happening and shoved Gabby toward the terrified female sales associate who was being held at gun-
point. He'd turned the attention on himself and saved
the woman and Gabby, but he'd gotten himself shot. In
the crossfire, the sales associate and Gabby had crawled
behind one of the counters and hit the alarm. Hearing
sirens, the robbers had grabbed what they could from
a smashed glass display case and fled.

Charlie had performed a heroic last deed. He'd died
on the stretcher a few minutes after Marla had arrived
at the scene. She'd been five minutes too late.

Five minutes. She often thought if she'd just been
there sooner, Gabby would have been with her and on
the way home.

Or, as her parents had stated, always trying to reas-
sure her, she could have walked in on the whole thing
and Gabby could have lost both her parents.

Marla leaned her head against the steering wheel.
She'd never told anyone, but the marriage had been over
long before her husband died. She'd told him as much
the day before he'd been killed. Now the guilt of knowing that, coupled with her guilt regarding her daughter's
trauma, was destroying her piece by piece. At least the

robbery perpetrators had been apprehended and sent to jail for the rest of their lives.

Her phone rang, startling her out of the dark thoughts that caused her to stay awake at night.

She grabbed her phone and saw her mother's name. "Hey, Mom," she said after hitting the answer tab. "I'm at the shop. I've got a few things to put away and then I'll be there."

"No, hurry, honey," her mother replied. "Gabby wants to tell you about how she and her pawpaw are out back playing golf—with Gabby's miniature set."

"Okay."

She heard giggles and then Gabby's voice. "Mommy, I wuv that golf car."

"You do? Are you and Pawpaw having a good time?"

"Uh-huh. When will you be here? You can ride with me."

"I'd like that. I'm on my way. About thirty minutes or so, all right?"

"Aw-wight. Here's Memaw." And her daughter was off again.

Coming home had been the right thing. Gabby had improved so much since they'd moved back to Millbrook.

Marla had to smile at the image of Gabby and Pawpaw riding around the complex. Her father had learned to play golf after they'd moved to the retirement village and now he loved the sport. Gabby liked watching out the patio door to see if Pawpaw would ride by in his funny little "car." So Daddy had found her a cute pink-and-green golf set. Marla's father was the only male Gabby would get near and even that had taken months to accomplish.

"He'll probably find her a nice pint-size golf cart next," she said to her mom, laughing.

"He's already on that one," Mom replied. "Why don't you rest up and then come for dinner? I'm making lasagna."

"Hmmm, that does sound good." Mom made the best lasagna. "Okay. I'll be there in about an hour."

"That'll work," Mom replied. "See you then—and you can tell me all about that Alvanetti wedding."

Marla laughed, ended the call and got out of the van to unload. Most of the time, she'd slice up the cake onsite and wrap it up to give to the family members, but today, in such a big place with so many plastered but skinny society girls, no one would dare ask for a piece of wedding cake to take home. And Mrs. Alvanetti and the groom's mother had both taken big slices and had saved the top layer for the couple's first anniversary, but had insisted on Marla taking the rest.

"Give it to a homeless shelter," Mrs. A had said with a Lady Bountiful smile.

"I just might do that," Marla had replied. But she'd take a couple of pieces for her parents and Gabby, too.

Then she thought about Alec Caldwell. He'd probably have his slice with a big glass of milk. With that close-cropped blondish-brown hair and those hazel eyes, he did look like the all-American type. The gung-ho all-around-good-guy type.

But not her type—at least not anymore. He might be out of the military, but his kind always looked for adventure. Plus, he had obviously been an upper-crust preppy, from what she could remember from hearing his name and background. So had her late husband. Charlie had been spoiled and pampered all of his life so he'd expected things to come easily to him. But he had saved Gabby and his employee.

Marla thanked God for that sacrifice. But she was afraid of moving on, afraid of getting involved with any man so soon after losing Charlie. Like her frightened daughter, she had been traumatized. Both by her husband's horrible death and by how horrible they'd both made their once-happy marriage.

But who was she to judge? She'd had a decent enough life growing up in Millbrook. Her college days in Tallahassee had been full of friends, and she'd been with Charlie, so it hadn't been all bad between them. At least Charlie had left a trust fund in his will for Gabby's future.

Marla shook her head and came back to the present again. What Alec Caldwell had done or did now was none of her business. She'd probably never have another encounter with the man anyway.

So Marla unloaded her supplies and finished tidying up around the bakery. Her two other employees had already gone home for the day, so she set the alarm and locked things up until Monday morning. Then she got in her van and headed southeast toward her parents' house. "Sorry, Soldier Boy. You're adorable and interesting, but I need to forget I ever almost ran into you."

Just as well. He probably had a society darling in his life anyway.

Chapter Two

Alec saw his friends sitting at a round table in the corner of the Back Bay Pizza House. Waving, he headed for the table, thoughts of Wedding Cake Girl as fresh as buttercream icing in his mind. He'd enjoyed that nice slab of cake she'd given him yesterday, but a good meal with these characters would cure him of any sugary feelings he might have. That, and the workout his physical therapist had just put him through an hour ago. He'd do anything to lessen the limp that slowed him down on a daily basis.

He didn't intend to mention that he'd met Marla Hamilton. His buddies were all bachelors, but lately they'd singled him out for blind dates and matchmaker testing. He didn't want to be the first one to cave.

"About time you got here," Detective Blain Kent said when Alec slid into a chunky wooden chair. "We're about to order."

"And he'll have a fully loaded meat-and-cheese, right?" Rory Sanderson, once an army chaplain and now a minister, said with a grin. "Am I right, Alec?"

The Back Bay Pizza House was famous for fat pizzas

that oozed with plenty of cheese and meat—or veggies, if you liked eating produce with pizza dough, which Alec did not.

"Right as rain," Alec replied with a grin. "And I don't plan on sharing."

Hunter Lawson, as always, didn't have much to say beyond a greeting that consisted of lifting a hand in the air. Former special ops, Hunter came and went so fast, half the time no one even knew he was around. A native of Oklahoma, Hunter hadn't decided if he liked Florida yet or not. He liked to wander around and sleep on couches. Definitely commitment-shy.

"So how'd it go with Mama Alvanetti?" Blain, a former Marine MP, asked after they'd ordered three loaded pizzas and their drinks.

Knowing that Blain's detective brain was always in overdrive, especially when it came to the slightly-on-the-right-side-of-shady Alvanetti family, Alec tried to tread lightly. "I finally got a chance to talk to her—after the big wedding yesterday."

Blain's blue eyes went dark. "It's always hard to pin down an Alvanetti. Did she agree to help fund Caldwell Canines?"

Alec nodded and waited for the waitress to pass their drinks around. "She did, but she was just finishing up with her niece's wedding and right after that, about to turn around and leave town for a while. I grabbed her generous check and got out of there."

They all laughed and moved on to other topics, catching up with baseball stats and anything sports-related. The four of them had formed a bond right here at the pizza house during a fierce game of darts, and after serving in the military, they'd migrated back to Millbrook Lake. They'd made friendships that would last forever; these weekly meals and the occasional fishing weekend out at the camp house they'd all bought together suited Alec just fine.

That bond extended to their faith, too. When they were about to leave, Rory, often called Preacher, turned to Alec.

"Hey, we're having this dinner at church Wednesday night. Kind of a singles thing, but more of a business thing. Thought I'd extend an invitation to you—but not for the obvious reason. The theme this week is local businesses and organizations."

"I certainly fill that bill," Alec replied, wondering what the catch was.

Rory grinned his boyish smile. "Thought you might bring some of your Caldwell Canines business cards and host a booth with your brochures, maybe even bring one of your service dogs. Good networking opportunities. A lot of other locals from all over the area will be there, and since we have a lot of returning vets around here…"

Alec mock-frowned but realized these kinds of events could help his cause. Plus, he hadn't been to church in weeks, and he missed the time spent with friends—even if his scar did scare some of the younger children.

"Let me check my busy calendar," he said. Then he laughed. "Sure, why not? I'm working the rounds right now, trying to drum up support, so it stands to reason that I need to attend an event that will bring Caldwell Canines more exposure."

"How are you doing?" Rory asked, with the concern only a pastor could exhibit. "You've missed a couple of fishing trips recently."

"I'm doing fine," Alec replied, glad to have Rory on his side. "It's been a process readjusting, but the foundation work is keeping me too busy to feel sorry for myself."

"Good to hear," Rory said, slapping Alec on the back. "You haven't been to church in a while, either. Maybe this will get you more involved again."

Alec rubbed a hand across his scar. "I scare people, Preacher. Especially children."

"No children at this event. Adults only." Then Rory leaned close. "I'm not judging, and I'm not trying to force you into anything uncomfortable. I really want you to share your philanthropic work with a few other people."

Alec thought about that. "I guess it wouldn't hurt to show people what I want to accomplish by placing disabled vets with service dogs. After all, that is the point."

Rory's grin widened. "So you'll come? Setup is around five. We'll do a reception type thing, with tables and booths for the vendors, and then we'll have a good home-cooked meal."

"I'll be there," Alec replied. "Just don't try to set me up with any women."

Preacher shot him a pained glance. "I have no idea what you're talking about."

Marla walked into the fellowship hall of the eclectic Millbrook Lake Church and started setting up the many platters and cake dishes she used to display and serve her cupcakes. Pastor Sanderson had called her last week to ask her about showing and selling some of her baked goods at Wednesday's single-and-social business-night get-together.

"You're not trying to set me up with anyone, are you?" she'd asked through a grin.

"Nah, just trying to get some networking going. Word of mouth is the best form of advertising and with your cupcakes, I'd say we'll give new meaning to that phrase. People will be talking with their mouths full."

"You are such a cutup, Preacher," she'd replied. "I'll be there. Thanks for inviting me. And this batch will be on me."

After unloading her serving trays and tiered plates she went back to the van to bring the first tray of cookies and cupcakes to the table where a placard read Marla's Marvelous Desserts. She and her staff had made around five dozen luscious little muffins in flavors ranging from Red Velvet Reality to Vanilla Velocity and Cinnamon Cream Cheese Calamity. She liked to name her concoctions to get attention. She'd even made a batch for Pastor Rory: Preachin' It Pecan Praline.

"Need some help?"

Marla turned from the creamy beige tablecloth to find Pastor Rory heading her way. The tall, relaxed minister was about as enticing as her cupcakes. He had shaggy sunshine-bleached blond hair, a boyish grin and blue-gray eyes that were always laughing. Most would think he surfed all day but this man did a lot of his surfing in the Bible. He was the best minister in the world. He'd sure helped Marla through some rough patches, but they were just good friends. Preacher liked tending to his sheep as much as she loved tending to her bakery items.

She nodded. "I have three more of these big covered pans out in the van. If you help, I'll give you a cupcake, no charge."

"I will accept that offer," he said, already walking backward toward the open door into the fellowship hall. "Even though I know you're giving them all out for free anyway."

She laughed and went back to her work, setting up her cupcakes on the platters and cake stands she'd brought in earlier and marking the flavors with cards one of her employees had printed out. Humming to herself, Marla got lost in arranging her presentation. She liked this part of her job almost as much as she enjoyed baking.

"Where do you want these?"

The deep voice behind her caused her to whip around so fast she almost knocked the whole table over. The man standing there holding a huge plastic-covered container was not Pastor Rory Sanderson.

Alec Caldwell smiled at her over the huge pan of sweets.

"Hello, Cupcake Girl."

So now she was Cupcake Girl?

Marla regained her equilibrium and smoothed the already-smooth tablecloth before she returned his smile. He really was a good-looking man, and that scar just made him mysterious and…intriguing. "Uh, hi, Soldier Boy."

He lifted the pan higher.

"Oh, just set it on the end of the table."

Alec did as she asked, then turned toward her, the clean scent of soap reminding her of wind and water. She noticed his slight limp and wondered if his leg gave him trouble. "So we meet again."

Alec glanced around the long room. "Yes. Small world."

Looking uncomfortable, he eyed the grinning pastor standing at another table. "Preacher seemed mighty keen on me bringing this in to you. Right after he told me you're single and that you're a good cook. Think we've been set up?"

Marla hoped the heat rising up her throat didn't show. "I don't know. Are you single and a good cook, too?"

He rubbed a hand down his scar. "Single, yes. Is that important?"

"You tell me, since you look so frightened."

Surprised that he kept glancing at the door, Marla shook her head and made a note of that panicked look in his amber-gold eyes. "I agreed to this event last week, but I never considered you might be here. And I haven't mentioned anything about being set up to anyone." Turning back to her table, she added, "Relax, Soldier Boy, you're safe with me."

"I didn't mean it that way," he said with a shrug and a sheepish expression. "Just a bad joke. Never mind."

She felt the heat now rising on her cheeks, the same kind of flush she got when she opened the door of a hot oven. "I mean, why would I mention you to anyone?" Then because that had sounded so very bad, she hastily added, "Not that I would mind mentioning you to anyone. I've just been busy. I mean, you're not on my mind."

Alec's brow twitched upward while his frown hardened. "Hmmm. I didn't tell anyone about our close encounter of the sugary kind, either, so let's both relax, Sweet Cakes. Preacher told me about this event on Sunday night, but he did remind me a lot of single people would be here."

Marla wished she could hide underneath the tablecloth. "So the preacher didn't know we'd already met.

We can't blame him for us running into each other again."

"Technically, no," Alec replied. "But you never know what runs through Preacher's mind. He just wants everyone to be happy."

"I'm such a ditz," she replied, wishing she wouldn't jump to the wrong conclusions all the time. "I'm sorry."

Alec stood back on booted heels, looking completely out of place with all the daintiness surrounding him. The trace of confusion in his eyes changed into something else…hope? "Maybe it was divine intervention."

Marla didn't know how to respond to that. She just stared at him for a moment or two and then said, "Or maybe because we both have kind of unique occupations, he honestly wanted to showcase our endeavors."

Alec glanced around. "Yep, lots of interesting artists and vendors here tonight. The butcher, the baker and the candlestick maker—"

She added her own nursery rhyme. "And rich man, poor man, beggar man, thief."

The smile on his face died a quick death. "I get your point."

Marla was definitely going to hide under the table. "That didn't come out right. I never was very good at nursery rhymes."

"It's okay," he said with a shrug but the darkness in his eyes told her it wasn't okay. "I get that this town thinks I was born with a silver spoon in my mouth. But I'm trying to honor my family's legacy. My mother's legacy, really."

"I'm such an idiot," Marla said. "Forgive me. I'm kind of nervous about this whole affair."

"I don't think you should call yourself names." He

stole a cookie off one of her trays. "You are neither a ditz nor an idiot, as far as I can tell. We're both nervous, but that doesn't mean we have to avoid each other."

"I do need to lighten up." She shook out her hair and took a deep breath. "I don't want to scare away any customers."

He relaxed at that, his hand moving over the scar on his face, a habit he probably wasn't even aware of having. "Yeah, tell me about it."

"I just did," she said. "But not in a very nice way. Can we start over?"

He grinned at her sharp retort but held out his hand. "I could use a do-over," he said. "Hi, I'm Alec Caldwell, Soldier Boy."

"Hi." She shook his extended hand, again feeling the warmth that tingled against her nerve endings. "I'm Wedding… I mean Cupcake Girl, at least tonight. Marla Hamilton."

"Nice to meet you," he said with a smile.

"So nice to meet you—again," she said, hoping they could be civil now.

He let go of her hand but kept his eyes on her. "Oh, and by the way, that cake was a-m-mazing. A-plus amazing. I might have to get married just to have that cake at the wedding."

She grinned at that comment and put images of him waiting at the altar for some happy woman out of her head. "I'm glad you liked it."

He gave her a thumbs-up and glanced around the room. "Do you think we're all single? I mean, it is singles night," he said. "All joking aside, are there a lot of single people in Millbrook?"

"Single-and-social night," she amended, wishing

he didn't make her so nervous. Her skin tingled with awareness while her nerves seemed to want to dance. "Networking with a spiritual twist—single or not."

"Then it *is* divine intervention."

Marla glanced around and noticed a lot of people. "I think you might be right." She lifted her hand toward a cute little older woman wearing a full skirt and pretty spring jacket. "Mrs. Braxton looks like a real cougar."

He laughed at that one. "She's got her own booth— showing off crocheted stuff from the Courthouse Collectibles. Lots of baby booties and a few nice feminine hats."

"Some men find that fascinating."

He shook his head but smiled. "And I guess that gray-haired man over there with the lovely seascape paintings would be just right for her?"

"Boston Bob? Of course. She can crochet him a good fishing cap and he can paint her sitting in the window, gazing out toward the sea."

Alec laughed out loud. "You have a vivid imagination. But you do have a romantic job."

"And you seem to want to go with the conspiracy-theory thing. What's involved with running the Caldwell Foundation, anyway?"

He put his hands in the pockets of his jeans. "Right now I'm trying to raise money for our Caldwell Canines Service Dog Association. We train and supply rescued dogs as service dogs for disabled veterans."

"Oh, that's amazing. I mean really amazing."

"Hey, that's my word. Find one of your own."

"Incredible," she quickly amended.

"You mean you never would have thought a rich-man type like me had a noble bone in my body?"

"I mean—" She stopped and looked at her shoes. "Yes, that's exactly what I meant, or maybe thought, but not anymore. I'm not doing very well at this networking thing, am I?"

He laughed and glanced around. "At least you're honest. That's refreshing." He nodded toward the other booths. "I guess I should mingle, huh?"

Marla warred with that notion. "I guess so." Relaxing a little bit, she glanced around. "Where's your table?"

He pointed two tables over behind her. "Right there. I'd better go finish setting up. Come over and see me when you have a minute. I have a vet coming with his service dog to show people exactly what we can do."

"I'll try," she replied, hoping she wouldn't have a minute, hoping she'd stay so busy she'd forget Soldier Boy. She didn't want to like Alec but something about his shyness and his wit made her want to get to know him. When she watched him walk away, his back straight in spite of that slight limp, Marla felt her heart turn as soft as marshmallow icing.

She could deal with the visible scars, but what if that handsome marine had the kind of scars that only came out when he was in a dark mood? And what if being around her brought out the worst in him, in the same way as it had her late husband?

She couldn't risk Gabby being scared into even more trauma.

And Gabby would always come before Marla's love life.

Chapter Three

Two hours later, Alec was exhausted but also glad that he'd come to the single-and-social event. He'd handed out a lot of business cards and had fielded a lot of questions about Caldwell Canines. His friend Wilcox had shown up with his service dog—a beautiful Labrador retriever named Rocket—right by his wheelchair. They'd both talked to the people walking around while Rocket stood by and did his job. People asked to pet him and Wilcox let them, but carefully explained how service dogs worked while they got to know Rocket.

"We got some donations, bro," Wilcox said once the line moved on. "You need to tell them about the school you want to build, too."

"Working on that," Alec replied. "Baby steps, Wilcox."

"I'm too impatient," his buddy grumbled. "And I'm ready for a good meal."

"I think it's about time to eat," Alec replied, his own stomach grumbling. But he did feel a tremendous satisfaction in seeing Wilcox so content after the turmoil of losing both his legs in battle. Rocket had been a big part of that contentment. The trained dog could fetch anything Wilcox needed, help him remember to take his medication and even alert him and calm him when an attack of posttraumatic stress was about to hit.

Now it was time for dinner and a short devotional.

Preacher walked up and nodded toward Alec while Wilcox trailed behind, still letting people pet Rocket. "I've heard only good things about you tonight." He waved to several others as they headed toward the food line. "You're using your resources to help others in need."

Alec glanced back at Wilcox. "Did you see the way Rocket protects him when anyone gets too close? He can bring Wilcox just about anything from a soda to his medicine. I want that for any veteran who needs it."

Preacher grinned and looked like a fresh-faced kid again. "Now you see what this networking stuff is all about. Like leading troops, but into a very different battle."

"I sure understand that," Alec replied. "Just hope I can keep fighting for the veterans who can't fight for themselves."

When Preacher got called away, he turned to search for Marla. She'd been pretty busy all night, too. Her display table was almost bare, and Alec didn't see her. Maybe she'd taken some empty trays out to her car.

"This was kind of fun," he said to Preacher when he returned. "Hey, where'd you find all these single people, anyway?"

"They're not all single." Preacher chuckled but his smile was triumphant. "But I did invite a lot of *available* people from other gatherings—the baseball park, the grocery store, the soup kitchen. I talk a lot, and single people volunteer a lot."

Alec shook his head. Rory Sanderson had his dream job. He'd seen death and war, but he'd always kept a positive, faithful attitude.

Alec wasn't so sure about himself however. "Does that make us generous or pathetic?"

Rory frowned. "Hey—nothing pathetic in lending a helping hand. But from what I've seen, when people are on their own too much they get lonely sometimes. It helps to find other people and do something good to contribute to the world around you."

"I guess I can't argue with that," Alec said. "I like volunteering, but I really need to focus on the foundation." At the look in Rory's eyes, Alec held up his hand. "I'm not saying I won't try to get out more, but I have to hit my stride, so to speak."

Preacher glanced toward Marla's table. "You might check with Marla about trying to hit that stride. She's always looking for help around her bakery, especially delivery-truck drivers." He crossed his arms over his chest and did that calm-and-relaxed thing Alec wished he could mimic. "You might have to get a special driver's license to make deliveries, but that's easy enough to do. And if you volunteer, you'll be helping her without making it look like charity."

Alec glanced heavenward. Was God trying to tell him something? Or was his friend trying to force him into something Alec wasn't ready for yet? "I'd have to think about that, Preacher."

Preacher caught on to his hesitation. "Your therapy seems to be working. The limp is less noticeable these days. The scar is improving every day, too."

"Yeah, the Florida sun makes the scar more pronounced but also helps it to heal, as long as I wear sunscreen," Alec replied, his hand automatically moving down the jagged edges of his wound. "I only remember it when I smile."

Rory punched him on the arm. "If you smile more often, you'll forget it's even there."

Alec doubted he'd ever forget this scar. Shrapnel right in the side of his face. He could still remember the intense, searing pain before he'd blacked out. His broken leg was healing but he'd always have this facial scar.

"Just smile," Preacher said. "I find a smile can put anyone at ease."

"I'll remember that, sunshine," Alec quipped. "Thanks, though, for being my spiritual advisor." They walked up to the buffet table. "I'm sorry I haven't been attending services much. I've been on the road a lot and I'm playing catch-up with all the board members and the foundation. I think it's called putting out fires."

Preacher waved to some people up ahead. "I know where your heart is, Alec. God does, too. Fellowship can help, but only if you're willing to let it help."

"I'm here, aren't I?" Alec asked, wishing Preacher wouldn't do so much preaching right now.

Oblivious to Alec's discomfort, Rory glanced toward Marla. "Listen, I saw you talking to Marla earlier after I sent you in with her trays, so I guess you two hit it off okay."

Alec didn't lie. "Yeah, we actually met briefly this weekend at the Alvanetti estate. She baked the wedding cake."

"Oh, yes, I forgot she baked the cake for the big wedding out there." Rory shrugged. "They used another minister for the wedding, but I'm cool with that." He ran a hand through his hair. "So…you met Marla— something you neglected to tell us at the pizza place."

"I purposely didn't mention her the other night. Didn't want to be grilled about it."

"Like I'm doing right now," Preacher said with a nod. "Okay, I'll back off. Anyway, since you two know each other already, would you mind sitting with her at dinner? She's kind of new to the church and…she's had it rough lately."

"How's that?" Alec asked, glancing over at Marla. She looked cute with her wheat-and-strawberry-colored hair up in a haphazard ponytail, and she seemed content in her own skin. But she did appear a bit standoffish and shy when her green-eyed gaze stared at the floor, instead of at him. Was she fighting her own battle?

"Not for me to tell," Preacher replied. "But she could use a friend."

"Are you setting me up?" Alec asked, resentment warring with gratitude in his mind. He didn't have time to explore a new relationship. Wasn't even sure he wanted to be in any sort of dating situation. So why was his best friend keeping after him? "You invited me here for more than just networking, didn't you?"

Preacher made a face and then lifted his hands, palms up. "Me? Never."

Alec wondered about that, but he couldn't turn down the request to sit with Marla at dinner. That would be rude—and besides, he did like Marla, whether she liked him back or not. He didn't want to make her uncomfortable, but…it was just a few minutes eating a meal in a crowded room. Maybe if he sat with his scar away from her, she'd be more relaxed around him.

Taking a small leap of faith and sending a prayer after it, Alec excused himself from the food line and strolled over to where Marla stood tidying her table. He'd keep things light and friendly in spite of the unfamiliar sensations tickling at his consciousness. No use in scaring her away, since nothing could come of this anyway.

"Hi," he said, his gaze moving over her cute blue button-up sweater and floral skirt. "How'd it go over here?"

"Good," she said, her eyes sparkling. "I think I drummed up some new clients. A wedding cake, a birthday party and an order of cupcakes and cookies for an entire kindergarten class. Plus, dessert for the Rotary Club meeting next week."

He liked seeing her smile. "Your treats will draw in a lot of people. I had a great night, too. I'll tell you all about it if you'll sit with me at dinner."

Marla looked around and then lifted her gaze to Alec. Did she want to eat dinner with him? Or did she want to bolt out the door? She glanced at the door and the buffet line before lifting her chin toward him.

Looking defeated, he gave her an out. "If you'd rather not, I understand."

She noticed the disappointment in his eyes, so she made her decision. She wouldn't be rude or give him the wrong idea, no matter what negative words came out of her mouth. No matter how her breath seemed to catch in her throat every time she was around him. "I'd be happy to eat dinner with you."

"Good," he said with what sounded like relief. "I

don't know a lot of people here, since I... I've kind of fallen back on coming to church."

"Why?" she asked while they walked toward the serving line.

The scents of chicken spaghetti and garlic bread made her mouth water while the nearness of Alec Caldwell made her heart go a little crazy. Which *was* crazy. She didn't react this way to men. She tried *not* to react to men.

"I shouldn't have asked that," she said, a hand going over her mouth. "I need to think before I speak."

He guided her into the line, his hand on her elbow. "I don't have any good excuses." He leaned close. "Except the obvious one. Sometimes, I scare little girls."

She glanced at his scar, her mind on Gabby. Would he scare her daughter? To keep things light, she asked, "Do you also scare big girls?"

His tiger eyes held hers. "Are you scared of me?"

Marla wanted to look away but not for the reason he'd stated. And besides, she gathered that question was a test. So she gave him a direct, sure glance. "No. I mean, that scar doesn't bother me. But...where you've been does."

"What do you mean?"

"War. Battle. Hidden scars. All the traits of a gung-ho man. Those things scare me."

He looked confused and shocked. "Wow. Tell me how you really feel."

"I like being direct and honest," she replied, her hand on the food spatula. Her appetite was suddenly gone. Since she didn't expect him to hang around too long anyway, she gave it her all. "I...was married to a real thrill seeker."

"You were married?"

Now it was her turn to be shocked and confused. "Yes. It happens."

He looked embarrassed. "I didn't mean to pry, but I'm not *that kind of man*. I mean, not the kind who pries and certainly not a thrill seeker. I was a good marine and I wanted to serve my country. Now I want to settle down and have a nice quiet life. No war, no battles, no underlying scars or regrets." He stopped in the line. "Wait, since we're being honest, I do have some regrets. But we don't have to go into that tonight."

Marla took the salad a volunteer handed her and found a table. She'd brought enough cupcakes to put one at every place setting—her contribution to the meal. She sank down and wished she'd kept her issues to herself. She was the scary one—blurting out the wrong things to a man she'd known for about five minutes. She was so not ready to date again.

After Alec slipped into a chair beside her, she turned to him. "I'm sorry. I shouldn't let my preconceived notions affect getting to know you. I'm sure you're a very nice person."

"Ouch," he said on a wry smile. "A very nice person is usually a person about to get the brush-off."

She should brush him off. She should get up and run screaming toward the door. But honestly, she couldn't see this man going off on her in a rage of anger or putting his fist through a wall to make a point. She couldn't picture Alec Caldwell falling in with a bad crowd just to make himself feel better, either. He was a friend of Rory Sanderson, and that alone was the best endorsement she could want.

"I'm only being cautious," she finally said, a fork in

her hand. "My husband and I had a volatile relationship. I can't put my daughter through that again."

"You have a daughter?"

Marla cringed and wondered why she'd bothered. Why was she telling Alec all the intimate details of her life? He probably didn't *really* want to settle down, and she surely didn't want to give him the impression that she was fishing for that very thing. She already had a bad history with men and she had a child, too. That child would always come first. Besides, he probably had some snobbish socialite to keep him company all the time.

She was used to seeing somewhat-interested men turn and walk away at this point, but Marla didn't want to put Alec in that category.

She reminded herself again that this was just dinner at a church function, not a first date. She could be honest with Alec and get it all out there, since nothing would come of this once they walked out the door.

"Yes, I have a child," she finally said. "Gabby. She's four years old and…special. My parents take care of her when I'm working or out doing things like this."

He took a quick sip of his tea and glanced back over at her. "If she's as cute as you, I'd like to meet her."

Marla almost choked on her chicken spaghetti. "What?"

"Don't look so surprised, Cupcake Girl. I like children. I actually used to be one."

Marla's shock turned to admiration. Alec made her laugh. That was certainly new and refreshing. But she couldn't let him near Gabby. So she pretended in order to hide the *clop, clop* of her beating heart. "I'm thinking you might still be one, at that."

He smiled and winked at her. "Want me to show you my spaghetti face?"

He moved to go for a handful of spaghetti, but she stopped him by grapping his wrist. "Don't you dare. I believe you."

But she couldn't believe he wanted to meet Gabby. He was obviously just being polite. Her daughter was adorable and well-loved, so Marla could handle most men walking away, but she wasn't ready to subject Gabby to anything too sudden, either.

While hearing this from Alec made her want to grab him and hug him, she had to push away that notion for Gabby's sake. Her daughter was still too fragile for a new man in her mother's life. Or in her life.

He leaned close, his eyes going smoky amber. "Well then, if you believe I'm still a kid at heart, can you believe that not all warriors are hard-core and full of rage?"

She swallowed and took a breath. "I'd like to believe that, but this is the part where most men get up and never come back."

He chuckled and pointed to his face. "This and my bad leg are usually the reasons most women never give me a second glance."

She took a sip of her tea. "I'm not good at believing things I can't trust. It's one of my biggest flaws."

"You can count on the truth from me," he said, his gaze holding her with a warm regard. "I'm my own man, and while I still have scars, I'm healing each and every day—even on my worst days. I just want the rest of the world to give me a chance. I want you to give me a chance."

Still not sure, Marla lowered her head and whispered, "What kind of chance?"

He held his hands up in surrender. "Just to be your friend, okay? So I can get free cupcakes and big slices of wedding cake, of course."

After that remark, he grabbed his fork and started eating his meal, his golden eyes twinkling.

Marla didn't know what to say to that eloquent declaration. She toyed with her tea glass and wondered what to do. Should she take a chance? Should she give Alec a chance—as a friend at least? He'd been nothing but kind to her, and he sure didn't fit the wounded-warrior stereotype, even with his visible scars still fresh. Maybe she should reach out to him—to help him on those worst days he'd mentioned.

Dear Lord, don't let me mess this up. She couldn't rush headlong into anything. She wasn't ready for that. But she could get to know him better, a little bit at a time. A friendship never hurt anyone. He was nice and he was working hard for a good cause. Wasn't that the best kind of friend to have?

"I'm willing to give you a chance, yes. But I need something from you in return."

"Name it."

"I need you to be patient while we become friends. I'm a widow with a little girl. We only just met, so I need to get to know you a little better before I can let you meet Gabby. I have to take things slow and be very sure of what I'm doing. She's been through a lot and… she's sometimes afraid of strangers."

He leaned back in his chair and studied her for what seemed like a long time. "I'm so sorry to hear you're a widow. Sorry for your loss, but happy to get to know you." Then he nodded. "No hurry. I'm not ready to dive right in to anything else, either. I've got all the time in the world, Marla. For you and especially for Gabby."

He lifted up the Give Chocolate a Chance cupcake by his plate. "Even your cupcake seems to be in on this little discussion. Everything in life involves either taking a chance or relying on our faith to see us through. As Preacher would say, it's the excitement of what's next that keeps us alive."

"Are you excited about…me?" she asked, too caught up in his words to care. "I mean about making a new friend?"

"I sure am. My new best friend is an amazing cook."

Then he bit into his cupcake and sent her a chocolate-covered smile that melted her heart.

Chapter Four

Two days later, Alec sat in his office inside the Caldwell house and finished up the last tasks of a long tempting spring day. Taking in the dark teakwood cabinets and matching desk, he reminded himself that this house had once belonged to his parents and their parents before them. His father had spent his childhood here and after his death, Vivian and Alec had stayed here with Grandfather.

Alec remembered his mother and grandfather had both grieved the loss of his dad, to the point that Alec was neglected and left to his own devices. But Aunt Hattie had taken charge and hired a housekeeper to cook and clean and help look after Alec. Because during some of those early days, his mother had refused to get out of bed.

He didn't like these memories, so he brought his mind back to the here and now.

The bay window off to the left gave him a perfect view of the big lake that fed into the Millbrook River. The river flowed south all the way into Escambia Bay and the Gulf of Mexico. Lots of fishermen and tourists came through here: some on their way home from having fun on the bay and some heading out to explore the balmy waters that poured out into the ocean.

But here, on the big oval lake that sat in the center of town, life moved at a slower current. The old umbrella-shaped live oaks and thick-trunked, waxy-leafed magnolia trees that circled the water made a nice shade for the blossoming hot pink azaleas and the thick clusters of gardenia bushes and hydrangeas that colored the manicured grass. White benches sat underneath the trees and along the trails that wound around the water. Ducks and geese quacked and cackled down near the lush orange and white daylilies growing near the shoreline. Occasionally out by the long pier, a fat mullet or a sleek catfish would jump up and make a lone splash in the dark water.

Alec got up and went to stand at the window—something he did on a regular basis every day since he'd come home. His loyal border collie, Angus, jumped up from his spot on the burgundy-colored Aubusson area rug and came to nuzzle Alec's hand. He patted the shaggy dog's head and nodded. "Okay, okay. I know it's time for our walk. Give me a few more minutes."

They had to wait until the sun began to set. His scar didn't stand out as much in the shadows of dusk.

Watching the ducks crossing the lake, Alec remembered paddleboats and picnics, racing boats and water-skiing all weekend long and so many other things that now seemed like sunny dreams. He'd had a good life. A life without a father, of course, but his grandfather had tried to make up for that.

He turned from the big lace-curtained window to stare up at the family portrait over the marble-encased mantel. His grandfather, Alexander Garrison Caldwell, stood dressed in a dark suit behind a high-back chair where Alec and his mother, Vivian, sat. Grandfather Alexander had insisted on having the portrait done only a year or so after Alec's father had been killed. Vivian pouted and fumed but she'd finally given in. Alec was around five and he was laughing up at his smiling mother. His mother's smile seemed frantic and forced while his grandfather's expression was full of indulgence and pride.

"We are a prideful lot," he said out loud.

"Talking to yourself again?"

Alec turned to find his Aunt Hattie standing at the pocket doors, her green eyes bright even if she did have cataracts.

"You caught me." He rushed to help her with the coffee tray. "Are we taking a break?"

"*You're* taking a break," she replied, ever the fussy hen. "I baked a pound cake and I have fresh strawberries from the Millbrook Market."

Alec did a mock glance at his watch. "I do believe I could use a break, even if it is near quitting time." He winked at Angus. "Sorry, fellow, our walk will have to wait."

"You'll need a walk. This might spoil your dinner."

"*You're* spoiling my dinner," he retorted but he sat down with her and took the chunk of buttery cake she offered him. "These strawberries look pretty tasty."

"Good crop this year, according to Delton Fisher," Aunt Hattie said, looking younger than her seventy years. Delton Fisher owned a large produce farm and he also managed a big farmer's market on the edge of town. He and Aunt Hattie, both widowed for years, were considered "good friends" around town. She shot Alec an inquiring smile. "Now tell me all about your day."

Alec grinned and refrained from teasing her about Delton. His aunt had lived here all her life. She'd married a local banker and lived down the street in a big two-story Georgian house until her husband had died six years ago. After that, she'd sold the house and traveled some before she'd returned to a smaller house across town.

When her sister Vivian had died last year, Alec had asked her if she'd like to move in with him, reasoning to himself that this house was too large and rambling for one person and that she was lonely and isolated on the other side of town. She agreed on the stipulation that he'd allow her to cook and clean the house.

"Cook, yes, and only when you're in the mood," he'd told her. "But I have a maid who comes twice a week to clean the house."

And so they'd settled in nicely together. His aunt didn't have a problem staying active. He rarely saw her most days. But on ones such as this, she'd take a few minutes to come into his office and check on him. He kept her apprised of Caldwell business and she kept him informed on the local gossip.

Now she sat back with her tea and smiled over at him. "You are a paradox, you know."

He took a big bite of strawberry-soaked cake and then gave her a questioning look. "Oh, and how is that?"

"Watching you now, I'd never know you were a hardened marine. You might be more comfortable in desert fatigues than you are here, but you *were* born to the manor, so to speak."

Alec had to wonder if he was truly suited for this duty. Sometimes he thought about what he'd like to do with his life, but for now he was focused on Caldwell Canines. "So are you saying I'm going soft on you, Aunt Hattie?"

She laughed at that question and reached across the side table to pat his bicep through his button-up shirt. "Are you?"

He waved a hand toward the stack of documents on the desk. "I'm fighting a different kind of battle these days."

"But the foundation is solid, right?"

He nodded to alleviate the worry on her beautifully wrinkled face. "Solid, yes. But I want to do more."

"You're still determined to build your training school? For the service dogs?"

"Yes, ma'am. It takes a lot of money to provide a service dog to an injured vet and most can't afford that cost. I want to be able to help any wounded warrior who can't afford to buy a service animal. And I've had several good contributions to match the foundation funding."

Aunt Hattie leaned back and crossed her hands in her lap. "Then what's wrong?"

"Nothing." He put down his plate of cake and sipped at the coffee. He couldn't explain something he didn't quite understand himself. But this restlessness had to stem from one thing. "I…I met someone—"

Aunt Hattie clapped her hands together. "Oh, how lovely."

He held up a hand at that feminine glee. "We're just friends, as per an agreement."

Aunt Hattie frowned and touched on her soft gray curls. "An agreement? That's not very romantic."

"I met someone," he began again. "She owns a bakery—"

"Marla's Marvelous Desserts?" Aunt Hattie's glee went into overdrive. "Marla is one of the nicest girls I've ever known. Her parents are a joy, too. And that cute little daughter of hers—"

"You know her?"

"Of course. I know everyone in Millbrook."

That was the truth.

His aunt leaned forward in her chair and clasped her hands together. "How did you meet?"

He told her about the wedding and the dinner at church. "Her desserts are…addictive."

"And she's a pretty woman." That knowing smile again.

Alec had to be careful here. "She's attractive, yes."

Like, cute-as-a-button attractive.

Aunt Hattie slapped a bejeweled hand against her lap. "I have a confession to make."

Alec shook his head. "You already knew all of this, right?"

His cagey aunt had plied him with cake and strawberries, hoping to get the real story. She, of all people, knew he had a major sweet tooth.

Giving him an innocent smile, she said, "Well, I might have heard a rumor that you two ate together at the singles dinner the other night. I would have been there, but Delton took me to see a play in Pensacola."

"Single-and-social," he countered. "Networking."

"Oh, is that what they call it these days?"

"It was a great networking opportunity. I've received

several donations from that one dinner and I've had several calls from interested people."

"And you've found a new friend."

He nodded. "Yes."

"Want to talk about it?"

"No, I don't. And please, I don't want you talking about it with all your church friends, either." He patted her hand. "I meet people all the time but Marla is…different. Let's just leave it at that, okay?"

"Okay, then. All in due time." His aunt took another nibble of cake. "But I'm so glad you're making new friends."

Bless her. She made it sound as if he was back in middle school, but Aunt Hattie would honor his wishes because she'd been raised to be polite and discreet. Even when she "shared" information with the other matrons in town.

Aunt Hattie didn't pursue the subject of Marla Hamilton, thankfully, and soon they were talking about the weather, his plans for the rest of the week and her upcoming doctor's appointment. Angus woofed and yawned and glanced longingly toward the window.

His aunt got up after they'd finished their cake. Alec stood, too. Aunt Hattie came around the coffee table and gave him a quick hug. "I'll see you later at dinner. We'll keep it light—just fresh sliced tomatoes and cucumbers and some cheese and crackers."

Then she glanced out the window and turned him around on his heels. "Oh, and by the way, your new friend is out there taking a stroll around the lake with her little girl."

Alec gave his aunt a frown but he moved toward the window in a flash, with Angus right behind him.

"You should go out there and visit with them," Aunt Hattie said, the hope in her voice shouting at him.

"I'd rather not," Alec admitted. "Not right now. Not yet."

"She's seen your scars, Alec," his aunt said on a soft note. "And Marla is the kind of woman who can deal with any scars you might have."

"Yes, she's seen my wound." He touched a hand to his face. "But her daughter hasn't. And she won't. Not until Marla thinks she's ready."

"I hope that's soon, then," Aunt Hattie replied before leaving him alone.

He turned back to the window and watched as Marla walked behind a bright pink-and-white miniature bike with training wheels attached. The little girl on the bike could be a tiny version of her mother from what he could see of her long reddish blonde hair. The sight of them together, laughing and having fun, tore at Alec in a way that nothing else had in recent days.

And made him ache for something unattainable, something unexpected.

Gabby looked adorable.

And so was her mother. Marla wore a flared floral skirt and a simple blue T-shirt. But her long hair spilled out around her shoulders in bright hues of gold and red.

Alec almost headed out with Angus, but he'd promised her he wouldn't push. And he didn't want to scare Gabby before they'd been properly introduced.

So he waited until they'd circled the park and when he didn't see them coming back around, he finally took his dog out for a lonely walk. For now, that would have to be enough.

* * *

Marla and Gabby left the park and headed back to Lake Street, but she couldn't help but think about the big white Victorian house that stood on a prime piece of real estate right across from the lake. Caldwell House had always been a fixture of Millbrook Lake, and she'd been by the old house many times through the years. But back then, she'd never connected the house with the man she'd recently met.

Funny how their paths had never crossed when they were younger—but then, Marla had lived outside of town on a farm and attended a different school from him.

Alec Caldwell had lived up there, in that wedding cake of a house, growing up. And now he was back as a grown man. A marine who'd served his country and was now trying to help wounded veterans have better lives.

What about his own wounds?

While Gabby had fed the fussy ducks, Marla had ventured a glance toward the rambling white house with the dainty scrollwork on the porch posts and the big bay windows on each floor.

And she'd wondered if Alec was in there, working hard at making his dream become a reality. Had he inherited a lot of money? Did he want the responsibility of running a massive charitable foundation? What had made him go from being a soldier to becoming a local businessman? Did he have another dream that he'd put on hold?

So many questions that she wanted to ask and so many questions that she needed to leave alone. Checking on Gabby, she watched her daughter and smiled. Gabby loved riding her bike through the park but she always stopped and waited for Marla if she saw any men approaching. Knowing that her only child was frightened of grown men broke Marla's heart, but as a mother, she stood between her little girl and any imagined dangers. Gabby was improving, though her therapist had told Marla it might take a while before Gabby got over her fears.

Which meant that Marla couldn't think about Alec Caldwell in any way other than as an acquaintance.

Because how could she bring together a man with a noticeable scar on his face and a child who had hidden scars that held her back? And how could Marla heal her own scars enough to even get up the courage to try?

She had to think of her child right now, and if that meant she couldn't go on a friendly date, then so be it.

After all, she wasn't ready for anything too heavy. She had Gabby and she had her work and she had friends and family to help her through. For now, that would have to be enough.

Chapter Five

Marla brushed at her hairnet and checked the fifty cupcakes she had baking for a birthday party out on the lake: twenty-five yellow-cake-flavored and twenty-five chocolate-flavored that she would turn into Suzie Sunflower Lemon and Cocoa Marshmallow Crème for a ten-year-old named Susan, who just happened to love sunflowers, chocolate and marshmallows.

"How we doing?" her assistant, Brandy, asked, her short hair spiked underneath her hairnet and her dangling gold earrings sparkling. "I have the yellow icing ready and I'm working on the chocolate." She glanced down at the pattern they'd created on the iPad. "Love the flower-shaped icing."

"About five more minutes," Marla said in answer to her question. She glanced at the clock. Almost eleven. "Mrs. Fontaine wants these by three since the party starts at five."

"Piece of cake," Brandy replied with a red-lipped grin.

That term was a joke around here. Marla laughed and hurried back to the sheet cake she planned to put in the oven next, for an anniversary party Sunday night at the church. White cake with cream-cheese icing and some colorful sparkles. The couple had been married forty-two years and they had five grown children and twelve grandchildren. They wanted the sparkles since they maintained they still had some spark in their marriage.

Marla smiled at that. She loved her job because, for the most part, she was involved in a lot of happy events—weddings, parties, showers and celebrations. Once, she'd even made cupcakes for a funeral—per a woman's three grown children.

"She loved cupcakes," one of the sons had explained. "She'd want us to have some at her memorial dinner."

Happy or sad, family was important. Marla was blessed to have her family nearby, but she did dream of having a special someone. Someone to hold and love, someone to make her laugh. Someone who knew she loved cookies and cupcakes.

When she thought of how those things had been sorely lacking in her own volatile marriage, she pushed away the guilt of not being a better wife and mother and went back to creating marzipan icing for the cupcakes. The mixture of sugar, almond paste and egg whites could be molded and formed into just about any shape or design. When the bell on the front door jingled, she glanced into the pass-through, expecting to see her mother with Gabby. Gabby had spent the night with her parents but was due here any minute to spend the day "helping Mommy."

But instead of her mother and Gabby, Hattie Marshall breezed in, her short salt-and-pepper curls framing her still-smooth porcelain face. "Hello, Marla," the older woman called with a chuckle. "It sure smells good in here."

Marla dropped the bag of powdered sugar she'd been measuring and headed out to greet one of her best customers. Miss Hattie loved to cook but when it came to desserts for big groups, she always ordered from the bakery. Usually over the phone and usually she'd send someone to pick up her orders. Marla only knew her from seeing her at the big farmer's market outside of town. Marla's parents used to run a booth out there during peak vegetable season.

"What a nice surprise," Marla said, glad for this short break. "What can I help you with today?"

Miss Hattie smiled and held a hand to her pearls. "I'm hosting the garden club this month and, since the gardens at Caldwell House are in full bloom, I thought I'd have an afternoon tea in the backyard."

Caldwell House?

Marla tried to hide her surprise. "Uh…okay. That's a nice idea but…" Then it hit her. "Oh, I'd completely forgotten that you and Vivian Caldwell are…were… sisters. I was sorry to hear of her passing."

Hattie nodded, a touch of sadness in her smile. "I know, honey. You've been away for a few years now so you wouldn't know the details. After my sister passed, my nephew Alec invited me to come and live with him at Caldwell House. He claimed he didn't want me living alone anymore, but just between you and me, I think he was the one who was lonely. Since I'm a master gardener and since I love to cook, I think he also wanted a feminine touch for the gardens and that massive kitchen." She shrugged. "You know that's a big old house and, well, he'd just returned from serving our country." She put a hand over her mouth. "And recovery from his injuries, at that."

Marla absorbed all of the intimate details as she suddenly understood why Alec needed a friend closer to his age. A doting aunt would be good company some days, but not so much at other times. But she did think it was incredibly sweet of him to ask his aunt to live at Caldwell House. "Yes, I guess I can see the logic of you moving in there with him."

Marla could also see the rather obvious reason Miss Hattie had come by to place her order in person. Nothing went unnoticed in a small town. Lately, Marla had ignored the local grapevine and focused on her work, but she needed to start paying more attention to the things happening around her.

Especially when this one particular thing seemed to involve her. In an unspoken way, of course.

Hattie Marshall took her time glancing into the glass display case. "I heard you and Alec met at that scandalous Alvanetti wedding."

"Yes," Marla said, checking behind her to make sure her small staff wouldn't hear. She didn't like gossiping about her clients. "I talked to him briefly after the wedding—"

"And gave him a piece of wedding cake," Miss Hattie interrupted. "He sure did brag about how good that cake was."

"Yes, well, I had plenty left over." Marla wanted to slink underneath the counter but at least Alec had mentioned her gesture. "I'm glad he liked the cake."

"And the cupcakes you served at that church function last week." Miss Hattie glanced around. "Marla, this place is adorable."

Glad that Alec's ditzy but sweet aunt had moved on, Marla took in the white wrought-iron bistro tables, the matching chairs and the soft blue walls lined with counters that held tempting desserts, breads and cookies. She'd found some inexpensive art pieces to grace the walls—a picnic scene on the beach and a Victorian-styled downtown scene that reminded her of Millbrook Lake. "I had a lot of help remodeling this place."

Hattie nodded and smiled. "I'm glad you've been so successful. But I've kept you long enough, so I'll get right to business."

And so they did.

Hattie Marshall ordered an array of tea sandwiches and iced sugar cookies, along with three dozen dark-chocolate and coconut truffles.

"I'll make the chicken salad since I'm famous for my chicken salad," she explained. "Oh, and I'll need you to deliver this the day of the party."

"Me, deliver to the house?" Marla asked before she could catch herself. Of course she delivered her own products. Sometimes because she didn't trust anyone else for the job.

"You do deliver, right?" Hattie's green eyes sparkled.

"Yes, ma'am." Marla would just send someone else this time. But with an order this big, she'd want to make sure everything was perfect—so she'd probably have to take someone with her and do it herself. How could she avoid that?

She hoped Alec wouldn't be around. Why would any man stay there with thirty women taking over the place? Besides, it was a big rambling house. She might not even see him at all. But what did it matter if she did run into him? They were…tentative friends.

Nothing more.

But Hattie Marshall's parting words spoke of something more. "I'm glad you and Alec have become acquainted. He could use a few more friends here in town since he's been away and well…he's a bit stubborn about getting out more." Then she held on to her designer purse and gave Marla a direct stare. "He needs to develop a new confidence and realize that people won't notice anything but his big heart."

Marla's heart opened at that comment. "I couldn't agree more, Miss Hattie. I do believe Alec has a good heart."

"I thought you might say that," Hattie replied. "I'll see you in two weeks…at Caldwell House."

Marla jotted notes and waved goodbye. "Thank you, Miss Hattie."

After Hattie had left, Brandy marched up to Marla. "Your cupcakes are cooling. Tell me, what's up with you and the Dream Marine?"

Marla couldn't hide her surprise. "Excuse me?"

"That's what all the girls around here call him," Brandy explained. "A dream of a marine—maybe McMarine. Yeah, I like that. A real hero with a mysterious scar. Like a pirate, but in a good way. Sigh."

Marla slapped lightly at her young, impressionable assistant. "He is a hero—he got that scar serving our country—but I don't have time to dwell on his other attributes. We've got to get these cupcakes iced and out the door."

Brandy grinned and started a singsong teasing. "You like him. You really, really like him."

"Hush," Marla retorted, a heated blush moving up her neck. "I don't even know the man. Back to work."

But she had to smile because she did like Alec Caldwell, the Dream Marine.

Really, really.

He now noticed her delivery van all over town.

He'd never made the connection before, but now it was kind of hard to miss the white van with the colorful confections glazed across the sides. Marla's Marvelous Desserts were beginning to haunt his dreams.

Alec didn't know why he couldn't seem to shake her but Marla's cute face was messing with his head. He had too much to do, so he needed to get his head out of the clouds and back in the here and now.

Today, he was on the outskirts of town standing on a now-vacant car dealership waiting to talk with a real estate agent. The real estate agent had been helping Alec scout possible locations for the Caldwell Canines training school and boarding kennel. This place just might do the trick.

Located in front of a big field, the massive building had been vacant for three years and the land behind it was also up for sale. It was away from any subdivisions and it was zoned commercial, so it was a perfect place to train animals. Plus, the main building would make a great training area, especially since they could build mock kitchens and other rooms to help with training any veterans who were in wheelchairs. Alec also hoped to build some dorm rooms and a large activity room, so veterans and others who needed service dogs could stay on-site while they trained.

All of this would take a lot of money and a lot of man power, of course. But the first step was securing the place.

Alec walked around the building, doing a preliminary check. When a sleek white sports car pulled up, he held back a groan. His Realtor had sent one of his newest recruits. Alec watched as Annabelle Banks took her time climbing out of her tiny car, all legs and blond hair as she curled and lifted her tall frame and then reached back inside for her huge designer purse.

Annabelle had grown up in Miami and she'd followed a military man to Northwest Florida. They'd parted ways after a few months. After being around her a few times, Alec could understand why. Some people just never adjusted to small-town life.

Annabelle was one of those people.

"Hello there, handsome," she called as she waved her red-tipped nails in the air. "I haven't seen you in a month of Sundays, you sly dog."

Alec motioned, pointing to his chest. "Who, me? I've been around."

"You've been hiding out in that gorgeous old house, is what I hear," she retorted as her high heels clinked against the hot asphalt. "I have my sources."

"I'm out in the daylight now," Alec replied. "And since it's hot out here, let's get inside." He glanced at his watch and refrained from telling her she was ten minutes late.

She knew that already. Just as she knew the asphalt wasn't the only hot thing out here—in her mind, anyway.

"Oh, stop frowning. You won't melt."

"I might," he replied with a smile.

Once they were inside, Annabelle went into professional mode. "It's a good space, Alec. Reggie thinks you'd be crazy not to make an offer. You can probably name your price. You know the dealership went bust and the owner had to take an early retirement. It's just sitting here empty."

"So I've heard." Alec wanted to make this place new again, to bring it back to life. He hated seeing vacant, run-down buildings all around town. But with the bad economy, there wasn't much anyone could do. Or maybe he had that wrong. Maybe he could at least try to bring life back to the outskirts of the town proper. If Lake Street could revive itself into a quaint little village on the square, surely he could do something about the strip malls and other commercial buildings.

"Whataya thinking?" Annabelle asked, her baby blues moving over his face with way too much interest.

"Let's take a look around and then I'll let you know," Alec replied, ready to get on with his busy day.

Annabelle giggled and walked him through the rest of the vast property. Alec had a few questions so she tapped notes in her mini-electronic tablet. About thirty minutes later, they were back outside and Alec hurried to open her car door. Annabelle dropped her bag in the seat, then turned and leaned on the door, her face inches from his.

Tossing her long locks, she gave him a brilliant smile. "When am I gonna see you at the country club again?"

"I'm not a golfer."

She leaned even closer. "I wasn't necessarily talking about golf."

Alec grinned and tried to back up.

And that was when he glanced up and saw the white van that chased him in his dreams. Marla's marvelous van made its way along the nearly deserted road. And Marla herself gave him a long, surprised glance before the van sped away.

Chapter Six

"You'll stay and have tea and sandwiches with us, of course."

The command was steeped in such a sweet smile, Marla wondered how she'd be able to decline Hattie Marshall's request. She'd planned for this delivery to be an in-and-out kind of thing. Just place the requested food in the huge kitchen and let the hired staff do the rest. Not that Marla minded helping out, since her name was on all the delivery boxes, but she didn't want to linger too long at Caldwell House.

"Marla, I insist," Miss Hattie said with that smile made of steel and sugar.

Marla didn't intend to cave, so she gave Miss Hattie her best shot. "I can't stay. I mean, I'm the caterer and I'm not dressed—"

Hattie took her by the arm and tugged her toward the big double doors to the back veranda of Caldwell House. "We're having this shindig out in the garden. You have on that cute sundress and you're wearing that glorious smile. You'll fit right in." Hattie leaned close and giggled. "I invited your mother, too."

Marla drew back. "You what?"

"I like your mother. Haven't seen her since they re-tired and moved to that quaint village out on the other end of the lake. Do you know, I used to buy fresh pro-duce from your parents at the Millbrook Market just about every Saturday during the summer? Their booth always had the freshest vegetables. Delton always speaks of them kindly and he sure misses doing busi-ness with them."

Marla didn't want to spoil Miss Hattie's memories by telling her that her parents had worked so hard in those days that they'd come home, collapse in their re-cliners, go to bed and then get up at dawn and start all over again. Or that she'd been in the back of the farmer's market, washing and sorting those vegetables on most summer days.

From picking the vegetables and carting them to the market to making sure they had help both in the fields and at their produce booth, her parents had loved their chaotic life. But it was a hardworking, common-people kind of life. Not a let's-have-tea-in-the-garden kind of life.

But Hattie Marshall meant well and she had always been sincere and straightforward. Plus, she was a loyal customer to Marla now. "Thank you, Miss Hattie. My mom doesn't get to enjoy such fancy occasions, but they have fun with their friends at the retirement village. I'm so glad you invited her today. She's always wanted to see Caldwell House up close."

"I'll give you both the tour once our other guests leave."

They were at the back of the house now. Marla had tried not to drool over the big, sunny kitchen with the industrial-size appliances, or the breakfast room with white wicker tables and chairs and a bay window over-looking the huge colorful garden.

She and her helpers had gone about their busi-ness, setting out the finger sandwiches, tea cakes and round creamy truffles on tables on the deep porch that wrapped around the back of the house.

Miss Hattie had covered two long tables with lacy white tablecloths and her kitchen staff had set out fine china—delicate teacups etched with yellow roses, matching luncheon plates and yellow-tinted goblets for the sweet mint-and-lemon iced tea. There was an urn for coffee and hot water for hot tea. Huge glass containers of water with lemon slices and strawberries floating in ice also graced one of the tables.

"Not too shabby," Brandy had whispered earlier while they were setting up. "We're uptown now for sure."

"Beautiful," Marla had replied. Then she'd shooed Brandy back into the kitchen to bring out the food while she directed the hired staff on how she wanted things to look for the best presentation.

Miss Hattie had thought of everything. She had sev-eral mesh oval and round food covers decorated with tiny flowers on their rims to cover the food. This was standard in the South, where bugs loved outdoor events as much as humans did and where no polite hostess would dare leave food out uncovered.

"Everything is ready," Marla said, her back to the open doors. "It's a great day for this. Sunny but not too hot."

"Perfect," Miss Hattie said, her eyes brightening at someone behind Marla.

Marla turned and stood face-to-face with Alec Caldwell.

Not sure what to say, she smiled and tugged at her ponytail. "Uh…hi." She'd managed to avoid him up until now but she'd heard some of the ladies commenting on how he'd escorted them to their tables. The man was certainly full of surprises—at first, a tough, buff soldier but then seeming to morph into a gentlemanly usher and escort.

"Hello," he said, his hand automatically raking across his scar. "That dainty food out there looks so good. I think we owe that to you, Marla."

His eyes moved over her face with each word, causing Marla to overheat in spite of the gentle breezes playing across the porch. "You aunt had a lot to do with that. I just followed her instructions."

"And she cooked up a wonderful luncheon for us," Miss Hattie replied.

"Speaking of that, I'd better check on the food one more time," Marla said as she brushed past Alec.

"And find your seat," Miss Hattie called. "I put you with your mother and two of her church friends."

"Thank you," Marla said, her heart pounding. What was wrong with her? Was she having some sort of panic attack? She needed to remember the last time she'd seen Alec. He's been standing in an empty parking lot talking cozily to a gorgeous blonde. Hard to get that image out of her mind, but at least it had brought her back to reality. He was off-limits to Marla.

"Are you all right?"

She whirled to find Alec behind her on the porch. Brandy pranced by with a smug smile, and two of the

extra staff members Miss Hattie had hired gave Marla
and Alec questioning stares.

Alec seemed to pick up on that, his hand touching
on the scar. "Let me take you to your mother's table."

Regaining some of her equilibrium, Marla shook her
head. She didn't want to make him uncomfortable. "You
don't have to do that. I shouldn't even sit down and eat.
I'm here to make sure the food is served—"

"No, my aunt has people to handle that. You *sup-
plied* the food, and while you're out there with the other
ladies, you can enjoy it. That way, you'll never know
I'll be in the kitchen snitching a couple of those little
women sandwiches and maybe some of Aunt Hattie's
chicken salad. And a truffle or two, of course."

Marla couldn't stop her giggle. "I'll alert the proper
authorities."

"No, no. My aunt is *the* authority around here. She
somehow convinced me that I needed to be polite and
escort the ladies, so if I have to suffer through this, then
so do you. Besides, she'd be appalled if she found me
sulking in the kitchen. Probably send me to my room
without lunch or dinner."

Aunt Hattie strolled by. "I heard that, Alec Caldwell.
And I'm glad you recognize my status. Now, go along
and steal some food. We have things to do here that
don't involve handsome, brooding men." Then she
winked. "Of course, we might actually talk about handsome, brooding men, right, Marla?"

Marla shrugged and hoped she wasn't blushing.
"Now you know what women really do at these functions. We try to figure out the male species."

"Well, all the best with that," Alec said. "But I will
take you to your table as planned." He glanced back at

his aunt. "Even though I'm a brooding, devastatingly handsome, wonderful example of the male species."

Marla didn't miss the sarcasm in his words. She could only imagine how uncomfortable he must have been earlier, being coerced to make small talk with a crowd of curious women. He was being overly considerate to insist on escorting her or anyone else to a table. And that was just it. Alec Caldwell had been raised to respect women and to be a gentleman. That was rare, and while she liked being independent, it was nice to be treated like a lady every now and then. She thanked God for that at least and lifted up a short prayer for Alec. *Let him see his worth, Lord.*

Alec had only agreed to help escort all the ladies to their seats because several of them were getting on in age and, as his aunt had pointed out in her charming way, "We don't need them falling and their orthopedic shoes going up in the air with them."

Of course not. He only hoped *he* didn't fall. His leg didn't hurt too much today, so maybe he wouldn't embarrass himself too much. But Alec had an ulterior motive for deciding to stay and risk people staring at his scar or giving him pitying glances. He'd wanted to see Marla Hamilton again.

Now he held her elbow in the way his mother and aunt had taught him from the time could walk and guided her to one of the round tables decorated with fat white magnolias and deep pink azalea blossoms.

"I'd like to meet your mother," he said. "My aunt knows everyone in town, but she speaks highly of your parents."

Marla smiled at that. "Joyce and Walt Reynolds. They know just about everyone in town, too."

"Except me, apparently."

"I'm sure they've heard of you."

He wasn't sure how to respond to that comment. Had her parents heard the gossip about him? About his injuries? Probably.

As if sensing his insecurities and doubts, Marla glanced up at him. "You're a returning hero, Alec. This whole town knows what you sacrificed."

He wanted to snap at her and tell her this whole town felt sorry for him, but that wasn't true. He just felt sorry for himself at times. But when he thought of how some of his buddies had come home in body bags, he straightened and thanked God he had an opportunity to start all over again. He would honor them by trying to be a better man.

"Thank you," he said, the burst of anger and regret lifting out in the wind that played through the old oaks.

They'd reached her table and so far, he hadn't said or done anything stupid.

"Hey, Mom." Marla leaned down to hug a plump older version of herself. Marla's mother had short blondish-brown hair with a few streaks of silver mixed in. But her eyes were the same spring green as her daughter's. "Have you met Alec?"

Her mother smiled and shook her head, her gaze moving over Alec with interest. "No, not officially, but he's been helping all of us to our tables, so we appreciate you, Alec."

Alec reached out his hand. "Nice to meet you, Mrs. Reynolds."

"Call me Joyce," she said. Then she introduced him

to all the curious women at her table. After the small talk had died down, she continued, "We love this garden. It was so thoughtful of your aunt to include me and insist that Marla takes a break and sits with her old mama. That's a rare treat for us."

He glanced over at Marla and pulled out the heavy white plastic chair for her. "Then I'll let you enjoy your luncheon. I know the food will be delicious."

Marla sat down and let him help her with the chair. "Thanks," she said again, her smile hesitant. "And get yourself a plate of food."

"I will," he replied. With a wave to all the women, Alec turned and hurried back to the house. His limp only reminded him that he couldn't move as fast as he used to, but in a pinch he could make a gallant escape. Escorting the women to their tables required going slowly, so that hadn't been so difficult after all. Getting away from his newfound feelings regarding Marla— well, that proved to be more of a problem than he'd considered.

Once he was inside, he leaned against the hallway wall and took a deep breath. Every now and then, he had sudden panic attacks that came out of nowhere. But with therapy, he'd learned to control them. So he took another deep, calming breath, and closed his eyes and focused on the image of Marla sitting in the garden with her mother.

A sweet image that did bring him a small joy. He often wondered what his life might have been like if his father had lived and if his mother had taken time to enjoy her life and her only son.

"Alec?"

He opened his eyes and stood up straight. His aunt

touched a hand to his face, over his scar. "Thank you, darlin'," she said. Then she kissed his cheek the way she'd done so many times when he was a boy. "Your mother would be so proud of you."

And with that, she breezed away, her floral dress swishing, her pearls glistening and her spine straight.

But Alec had to wonder. *Would* his mother have been proud of him?

Chapter Seven

❧

"Your house is amazing."

Marla had packed up the last of her supplies and helped the hired staff put away the leftover luncheon food and tidy up the kitchen. Thankfully, she'd calculated a good amount with no waste. Her food had been a hit, and she'd received several requests for her business card.

Silently sending up a prayer of gratitude, she had to admit the highlight of this day had been the private tour Alec and his aunt had given Marla and her mother. Caldwell House was three thousand square feet of Victorian charm, with five bedrooms and four bathrooms, a large office and den, a sunroom that served as an extra dining room and a formal dining-room-and-living-room combination. Not to mention this kitchen and all the bay windows that brought in light on both floors. She'd love to curl up with a book and some hot tea near one of the windows. She'd found charming nooks that allowed the sunshine to pour in and also highlighted a good view of the lake.

"Thank you," Alec said now. "And thanks for leaving me that huge plate of leftovers in the fridge."

They were alone together in the kitchen. Miss Hattie had insisted on taking her mother out to the greenhouse to give her some cuttings from her prized angel-wing begonia.

His dog, Angus, brushed up against Marla's leg and she leaned down to pat his thick golden fur. The dog had been allowed out of Alec's office after all the other women had gone home.

Alec called Angus over and offered him a treat from a jar on a small counter by the back door. "I think my loyal companion has his eye on one of those cupcakes."

Marla gave Angus a questioning glance. "He's not allowed, but the least I could do is to leave you and Angus some treats, since you've been a walking advertisement for me since I gave you that piece of wedding cake."

His gaze held hers, his smile comfortable and self-assured now. When he smiled like this, Marla hardly noticed the jagged scar along his cheekbone. "I know a good thing when I see it."

Marla didn't know what to do with her hands since she'd packed everything up and even loaded the van. She'd sent Brandy home early, but she intended to run by the shop to unload and wash up her pans and utensils—her way of unwinding after a day's work. Gabby was with Marla's dad, riding around on the golf cart—another step in her daughter learning to trust again—but her mom had promised to hurry home and round them up for a light dinner. Marla would meet them there.

"The luncheon was really nice," she said, nerves clanking like spoons inside her stomach. "I know my mom misses her garden, so she'll appreciate the cuttings Miss Hattie's giving her."

"Do they like the retirement village?" he asked, his eyes a rich amber in the late afternoon light.

She laughed. "They love it. I mean, we lived on a farm and our neighbors were miles away. I thought my dad would hate the close, tight-knit patio homes, but he's in charge of the community garden and he's on the homeowner's association board. My mom is thriving, too. She's in a quilting circle and she loves going on the shopping and beach excursions the ladies have each month. They go out to dinner and they often have big cookouts at the clubhouse. I think they've both taken up water aerobics in the pool, too."

"I'm glad they're happy, then." He rubbed his scar then shook his head. "Maybe I should encourage Aunt Hattie to join in some of the events, if that's possible."

Marla glanced out the big window over the sink and saw her mother and Miss Hattie laughing as they strolled through the garden. "The activities director— Cindy—encourages bringing guests since she considers them prospects for residency one day."

He grinned at that. "Aunt Hattie might surprise me and move out there. She's threatened before."

"Do you like having her here with you?"

"I do," he said. Leaning into the marble counter, he stared out the window. "My mother never recovered from losing my father and, well, unlike her sister Hattie, she didn't like group events. Aunt Hattie knew how to deal with my mother's mood, so she was always around when I was growing up. It's only natural that the two of us share this big house. Plenty of room for Angus and us."

Marla remembered Vivian Caldwell as being an attractive, elegant woman who had a mysterious, aloof air about her. She always made the paper on the society page, however. "But your mother was active in the community, right?"

"Yes, but on her terms," he replied, his expression full of a deep sadness. "She contributed a lot of the Caldwell money through the foundation. She didn't like getting her hands dirty but she was generous."

Marla wondered about him. Was he as reclusive as his mother? It seemed that way at times, but he'd been nothing but charming and accommodating today. "And do you like getting your hands dirty?"

"I don't know yet." He shrugged. "I'm used to being down and dirty on the front line, but it's a different thing now that I'm home and out of the military. The foundation keeps me busy and trying to start this new venture with the Caldwell Canines is a challenge. But I've always liked being hands-on."

Marla was happy to hear that. "Well, my dad's certainly looking for able bodies to help with the garden out at Millbrook Lake Retirement Village. Most of his friends have to be careful of overheating or hurting their backs."

Alec came around the counter, his smile making her forget all about her vow to keep him at arm's length. "You have my number. Tell him to give me a call anytime. I have three buddies who can do everything from hoe a row to get cats out of trees."

Marla loved his sense of humor and she was glad he had buddies. Knowing that made him more accessible for some reason. "And I'm guessing Preacher Sanderson is one of those three?"

"He's at the top of the list. I met him when I was recovering stateside. He was more than a chaplain in the army. He's good at everything he tries."

"He's good at helping people who've lost hope," she said before she could pull the words back.

"Did he help you?"

"Yes." She glanced down at her hands and wished she'd stayed quiet. "He wants to help Gabby but she's still shy around him." Giving him a quick glance, she added, "She's uncomfortable around most adult men. Her therapist says it'll take a while for her to heal."

Alec leaned in. "I understand that concept. I had a hard time when I finally came back here. I was the same but different. Sometimes, it's difficult for others to understand that soldiers go through a lot they don't like to talk about. I would imagine children have it even harder when they're dealing with trauma. Anyway, I hope I get to meet Gabby one day, but no rush on that. Preacher helped me work through things, and I still have bad days."

She wished she could ask him about those things, but Marla didn't want to pry. He'd tell her if he wanted her to know.

"I'm glad you had a friend."

"Yeah, so am I." He took her by the arm. "Let's get out there and see what those two are talking so intently about."

So that ended the conversation. It seemed neither of them wanted to talk about the past or their hidden scars. Marla accepted that maybe they both were a little shy in the getting-to-know-you department.

To lighten the mood, she glanced out the window. "I think maybe they're discussing the hibiscus plants?"

He winked at her. "Either that or…maybe they're comparing notes on you and me."

She laughed at the teasing look in his eyes. "Do you want that?"

"Not really," he said as he guided her out the French doors. A nice spring breeze played through the palm fronds on one side of the yard and tickled along the broad porch. "I prefer speaking for myself."

"Same here," Marla said as they moved down the steps. "But you know they mean well."

"I do. Meaning well can often lead to misinterpretation, however." He stopped before they reached the gazebo where his aunt and her mother had settled. "I'd never want you to hear something about me that might upset you."

Before she could respond, her cell phone rang. "It's my dad," she said to Alec.

He nodded. "Go ahead. I'll see if these two have figured out a way to solve world peace."

Marla answered the phone on the second ring. "Daddy, hi. Is everything okay?"

Her father sounded winded. "No, honey. But don't panic, okay? Gabby is a little upset is all."

"I'm on my way," Marla said, her stomach knotting. She motioned toward her mother but kept speaking to her dad. "What happened?"

"Dipsey McQuire. He saw us on the golf cart and waved. When we got closer he tried to tickle Gabby's tummy. Gabby got scared and grabbed hold of me. I guess his red beard threw her a bit. She's all right, honey. But she's asking for you. I can't get her to calm down."

"I'll be there soon, tell her. Okay, Daddy, tell her I'm

coming." Marla ended the call and hurried toward her mother. "Gabby got scared, Mom. Mr. McQuire tried to talk to her."

Her mother put a hand to her mouth. "Oh, no. He's harmless but he's got that big beard and he laughs so loudly. I'm sorry. I told your daddy to stay on the less-traveled trails."

"What can I do?" Alec asked, clear concern in his eyes.

"Nothing," Marla replied. "I… I had planned to take all of the leftovers and my equipment back to the shop."

He stared at her for a minute and said, "Give me the keys to your van. I'll go to your shop and unload it."

Shocked, Marla shook her head. "But you don't know the code to get in."

"Can I call someone to meet me?"

"Brandy," she said. She spouted out the number.

"Got it," Alec said, writing the number on his hand with a pen he'd pulled from his pocket. "Brandy and I will take care of the shop. You go with your mother."

Marla didn't know what to say. "Thank you, Alec."

Aunt Hattie walked with them to a side gate. "I hope your sweet girl is all right, Marla. Poor little thing. We'll send up prayers for her healing."

"Thank you," Joyce said. "We had such a nice time."

Aunt Hattie hugged her mom. "Come back again, please."

Alec guided them toward where her mother had parked on the side street. "Call me when everything is okay," he said. "Brandy and I will make sure the van is cleaned out and your shop is locked up tight."

Marla could only nod as she and her mother hurried to her mother's car. When she glanced back, Alec was already in the van. He shot her an encouraging smile and waved her on.

Marla turned around to stare straight ahead, her purse clutched in her hand. Worries about Gabby being afraid warred with the tiny crack in her heart at the way Alec had offered to help her.

"He's a very nice man," her mother said.

"Yes, he is." Marla couldn't quite believe that Alec had taken control without batting an eye. Then she gave her mother a reluctant glance. "Once a marine, always a marine, right? He must have taken control like that in much worse situations."

Her mother patted her hand. "Right. We women like our independence but sometimes it's nice to let others help us when we really need it." Then she shot Marla a knowing motherly smile. "Especially if the help comes from such an unexpected place."

Marla would have to remember that sage advice. Had she become so closed off and out of touch that she'd forgotten to accept kindness? Especially the kind that left her surprised and touched?

Alec couldn't get the memory of Marla's panicked expression out of his mind. Glancing at the clock again, he noted that three hours had passed since she'd left with her mother to go and check on Gabby. What had happened?

After getting in touch with Brandy and explaining that he needed her help, she'd met him at the shop and together they'd put away Marla's supplies and the remaining food.

"We sometimes take any fresh leftovers to the homeless shelter on the other side of town," Brandy had told

him, her tone still a bit uncertain at having him helping her. "Marla also donates any pastries that are left
but still fresh."

Feeling like a clumsy giant inside the dainty little
pastry shop, Alec had been careful not to break anything. But tiny Brandy had rattled dishes and slung pots
as if she were a navy cook. Alec liked the young girl
with the auburn-colored gamine haircut and decided it
was probably fun to work in a place like Marla's Marvelous Desserts. Who didn't have a sweet tooth, anyway?

After they'd finished, Brandy had offered to give
him a ride home. But Alec had thanked her and de-
clined. He'd decided to walk home since it was only
about a half mile.

Right now, he was late for pizza with his buddies out
at the fishing camp that they'd all bought together. He
wanted to call Marla but Alec didn't think they'd ad-
vanced to the point that he could do that. She seemed
as skittish as her little girl.

Maybe, like Gabby, Marla was afraid of getting too
close to any man who might do her harm. Wishing he
could help heal the little girl, Alec wondered if he'd ever
get to meet Marla's daughter.

Or if Marla would ever allow him to get closer to
her. She had yet to explain why her daughter was so
frightened of men.

Did he want to get that involved? To get closer to
Marla and Gabby? Maybe he should be thankful since
he didn't want to risk upsetting either of them.

When the phone rang, he breathed a sigh of relief.

"Marla, hi. I hope everything's okay now."

She let out her own breath. "Crisis averted. She was

mostly tired and needed a nap, but Mr. McQuire is a tad too jolly and friendly for her right now. Sometimes Pawpaw forgets to be stern with her regarding nap time so they'd stayed out on the trails too long."

"How was she when you got there?" Alec asked, his heart turning to putty for the little girl.

"Crying, but my dad had given her a grape Popsicle and she had it all over her blue T-shirt and once-white shorts. After we washed her off and changed her clothes, I read her a story and she fell asleep. She'll be out for the night so Mom's letting her sleep here."

"So you'll come back to town?"

Silence. "I don't know. Brandy said you were a real trouper with helping get the shop in order, so I don't have to worry about that. Thank you again, Alec."

"Thank me over dinner," he said, wondering how he'd found the courage.

Silence. "I don't know…"

"Just dinner, Marla. Unless you'd rather stay near Gabby."

"My mom's offered to cook dinner, but I'm not that hungry."

"Then I'll come and pick you up. If you don't want to eat, I'll take you home. Or we could go for a stroll around the lake."

She didn't speak and the seconds ticked off until Alec felt sweat popping out on his brow. "It's okay. Never mind."

"A stroll would be nice," she said. "Give me a half hour to freshen up."

"I need your parents' address," he said before she got away.

Marla gave him the house number. "The one with the magnolia tree in the front yard."

"I'll be there soon," Alec replied. Then he stared at his phone and wondered if he'd taken the right step.

Looking down at Angus, he said, "Guess I'll have to give the guys a rain check, huh, boy?"

Angus woofed in the affirmative.

The guys would certainly give Alec a hard time once they found out he'd ditched them for a date. But for once, he didn't care about that.

Chapter Eight

"Mom, people are staring into the dining room window. What have you told all of your friends?"

Marla saw the flash of a grin on her mother's face, followed by a big-eyed innocence. "Whatever are you talking about?"

And she knew that polite evasive technique, too. "I'm talking about Alec. Did you call the neighbors the minute I told you he was coming out here to get me?"

"To take you on a date," her mother countered.

Marla saw the bevy of senior-citizen women gathering in the early evening sunshine in her mother's small backyard. "And tell me again, what kind of meeting did you *suddenly* remember?"

Joyce eyed the clutter of females bringing their iced-tea glasses and finding seats on the porch furniture. "Well, I took a walk after we got Gabby to bed. When you were on the phone with Alec, I might have mentioned that I made a peach cobbler yesterday and I might have invited several of my closest friends to come by and have some with the homemade ice cream your daddy made this afternoon after he had his nap and now we're having what we call a 'sudden supper.'"

"Mom, we've already had supper."

"Oh, we just call it that to make it clear that it's nothing fancy."

"Right." Marla checked her hair in the hallway mirror and then waved cautiously to the half-dozen women giggling and teetering on the porch. "They must really like peach cobbler."

"Oh, we all do. With ice cream. I wonder if Alec would like to stay and have a bite?"

"I think he would," her dad said from the front door. "I just invited him to come on in since I didn't think you were ready yet."

"Arrgh! What if Gabby wakes up?" Marla hated to grunt like a pirate, but her parents were so obvious a squirrel could guess what they were up to. "I won't show him off like some prized vegetable," she said, only to turn around and find Alec smiling at her from just inside the front door.

"Hi," she said, thinking this little patio home had just become even smaller. Her dad kept the front door so greased it didn't squeak or creak enough to warn a person that someone was entering the premises. That could be dangerous.

Right now, it had become very dangerous. Her heart turned up the beats while her skin turned as pink as her mother's prized geranium blossoms. She only hoped Gabby didn't wake up and find him here. She'd planned to meet him outside, but now he was here, inside, and giving her a questioning smile.

"Hi," he said back to her, looking good in a black

T-shirt and faded jeans. "Somebody mentioned peach cobbler so here I am. Hope you don't mind."

"Of course not," her dad interjected.

"Come in," Joyce called on a sweet note of hospitality. "Good to see you again, Alec."

"Good to see you again, Mrs. Reynolds," he replied, an amused grin making him look way more tempting than cobbler and ice cream.

"Nice to see you, too," her mother responded, her eyelashes fluttering like a teenager's.

Honestly.

Marla wanted to run into her room and slam the door, but since her daughter was asleep in the extra bedroom, that couldn't happen. She'd just have to make the best of this and remember to never, ever again bring a man into her parents' home. Ever.

Alec gave her an appreciative once-over. "If you think peach cobbler will ruin my dinner, I can assure you I'll be ready to eat again in a little while."

"It's fine," she said, her own stomach too keyed up to even think about food. "Come on in, but be forewarned— this place is not for the faint of heart."

"I think I can handle it," he said. And then he noticed the women craning their necks at the big window by the Florida room. "Uh, am I interrupting some sort of meeting?"

"Don't ask," Marla said on a long hiss. "Just eat your cobbler and ice cream so we can get out of here."

"Will they hurt me?" he whispered against her neck.

Marla almost forgot her shame and embarrassment. "I'll stay between them and you, don't worry."

Alec waved to the women, causing them to scatter

like a flock of colorful birds. "And here I thought retirement homes were boring."

"Never a dull moment around this one," Marla retorted.

"Okay, everybody out on the porch," her father announced, his churn of homemade vanilla ice cream in
tow.

"I am so there," Alec said to Marla. And again, a
shiver went down her spine—a shiver of anticipation,
of some sort of awakening that both frightened and intrigued her.

"I'm going to go and make sure the door to Gabby's
room is shut," she said. "I'll be right there."

Assured that Gabby was down for the count, Marla
hurried back to find Alec, now oblivious to their fas-
cinated audience of arthritic admirers. But when she
got to the door, Alec was still inside. He hesitated, his
hand going to his face.

The scar.

"Do you want to leave?" Marla asked, her heart doing
that thing that made her feel as gooey inside as one of
her Marshmallow Marvel cupcakes.

"I don't want to be impolite," he said, a look of dread
scattering across his features. "What should I do?"

"Smile," she said, her hand on his. "That should do
just fine."

"Are you sure? I mean, I only recently starting trying to get out more. I don't want to—"

"Alec?" Joyce stood with her hands clasped together.
"It's going to be okay."

Marla wanted to hug her mother for being so thoughtful and sensitive. But then, her parents had learned how

to deal with this kind of thing since Gabby had her own bouts of fear and shyness.

Alec gave Marla a questioning glance and turned back to her mom. "Okay, then. Take me to the peach cobbler."

Marla breathed a sigh of relief. It would have been much worse if they'd turned and left. But somehow this big, brave marine had just taken another piece of her heart by showing his deeply anxious side twice in the same day. A side with which she could certainly identify.

After he'd been introduced to all of her mother's friends, Alec relaxed and managed to become the charming man who put on a public persona in spite of his wounds. When one of the women thanked him for serving his country, he looked embarrassed and confused.

"Just doing my job," he said in a low voice.

Marla's dad changed the subject to fishing and growing vegetables. While the women got going on that subject, Marla gave him a quick glance. "Ready to get out of here?"

Alec nodded like a kid sitting in the principal's office. "Please."

"Let me go check on Gabby again and give her a good-night kiss," she said. She left him talking to her parents and their friends about which vegetables they liked most.

Gabby was snuggled in with her favorite stuffed animal, a bright green grinning alligator she'd named Allie. Marla kissed her daughter's sweet-smelling cheek and thanked God for the honor of having a child to love. She couldn't mess with Gabby's fragile state right now by bringing a strange man into their lives. Sure, Gabby was getting better every day and sure, Alec was so different from any man she'd been around lately—and very different from her late husband—but Marla just couldn't see how the future would pan out right now.

She had to protect her daughter.

She also needed to accept that she liked Alec and wanted to get to know him better.

But how did she balance the two?

Standing at the door, she watched Gabby and heard her daughter sigh in her sleep. When she came up the short hallway, Alec was waiting, his hands in the pockets of his jeans. He looked both out of place and completely normal, standing in the tiny room.

"Everything okay?"

"Yes. She's out for the night."

They thanked her parents, said goodbye to the moon-eyed ladies who stared after them and then giggled all the way to his car.

"Wow," Alec said as he started the purring engine. "That was some kind of ambush."

"I'm so sorry." Marla put her head in her hands and shook her head. "I haven't been this mortified since junior high."

Alec drove through the crepe-myrtle-draped drive leading back to the main road, where a lighted sign surrounded by palm trees announced, Welcome to Millbrook Lake Retirement Village.

"Remind me to never bring you out here again," Marla said.

He actually laughed but the sound was filled with relief. "Hey, your dad had me at peach cobbler, but I...I almost panicked there for a second. I mean, I didn't want to upset Gabby or her mother."

And Marla had thought he was worried about his scar.

"You were great," she replied, proud of him and touched that he'd thought of Gabby and her. "And they might be overly curious, but my mom's friends are kind and understanding, too. And very patriotic."

"They were nice." He glanced over at her. "Your father invited me back to help pick vegetables next week."

"Oh, no. Don't let them draw you in like that. They might not ever let you go."

"Hey, I don't mind. My buddies keep telling me I need to just be myself and quit worrying about the scar or the problem with my leg."

Marla knew that was good advice. "Your limp doesn't seem pronounced as it was when we met at the wedding."

"I'm getting better every day and my doctor gave me the go-ahead on driving again about two months ago, but some days it really bothers me." He shook his head. "And going to a wedding as one of my first big outings didn't help matters. I was rushing to get out of there when I…ran into you."

Marla liked the way he hesitated on that. Did meeting her have that kind of affect? The same way she felt each time he walked into a room, that feeling where she had to catch her breath?

"Do you go to physical therapy?" she asked to keep things on an even keel.

He nodded, maneuvered the car out onto the road back to town. "About two days a week at a big complex near Pensacola that specializes in PT and pain management. I visit with some of the other wounded veterans and offer them help."

"Do you have a lot of vets who need pet companions?"

"More than we can service." .

"What can I do?" she asked, wanting to help.

He looked surprised and then pleased. "We're always looking for fund-raisers to raise money to help pay for the high cost of adopting and training the animals. Not to mention volunteers who help with maintaining the animals."

"I'll figure out something," Marla replied. "Maybe something out at the village? A cookout, or picnic."

"Are you asking my permission?"

"Just checking to see if you ever want to go back into the senior-citizen fray."

"Of course I do," he replied, his eyes dark in the night. "If I can survive today—two events with a lot of females, including my Aunt Hattie, your mom, your mom's friends—well, I think I can survive just about anything."

Marla relaxed back against the smooth leather seat. She liked this man and that surprised her. Alec wasn't an adrenaline junkie who lived for the thrills in life. He was an honest, good man who'd made a decision that went against the lifestyle he'd been accustomed to by joining the marines. That must have hurt his mother tremendously after she'd lost her husband to the military and Marla suspected he was still suffering from the guilt of that. But he had survived and he was home now and trying to help others.

She could so easily fall for Alec Caldwell. But she

needed to remember one very important thing before she let down her guard.

Her daughter might not ever be able to accept another man in her life—or at least any man besides her grandfather.

And if that meant Marla couldn't have a relationship with Alec, then she'd have to walk away. She wouldn't risk her daughter's well-being for anyone.

Not even a handsome hero.

Chapter Nine

～

Since they'd both had big bowls of cobbler and ice cream, Marla and Alec decided to forgo eating dinner and instead just bought two carry-out cups of fresh lemonade from the Millbrook Fish House.

"Still want to walk around the lake?" Alec asked after parking his car near the garage at his house and wondering if she was tired of him already. "You've been kind of quiet since we hit the city limits."

"I'd love a stroll," she said, her smile not making it all the way to her eyes. "It's been a long day."

"Are you tired? You had a *busy* day."

Marla played with her straw. "Yes, but I'm also wound up so I'm hoping a walk will do the trick."

"Okay, then."

They started toward the circular sidewalk, which wrapped around the water like a silver snake. Up the path an ornate footbridge crossed over where the lake merged with the river that ran into the big bay. Alec did a visual sweep of the area, glad that only a few people were out tonight.

"Don't you usually take Angus for a sunset walk?" Marla asked, glancing back toward the house.

Alec turned toward her. "Yes, but he doesn't have to walk every time I do. I thought he'd demand all of your attention so out of pure spite, I left him behind."

"You wouldn't do that to Angus, right?"

She frowned her way into confusion, causing Alec to let up and give her an amused smile. "No, but he does demand a lot of attention."

"I don't mind if you want to go back and get him," she said, obviously still not sure of his sincerity.

Was she looking for an excuse to stall him? No, he was probably just imagining things.

"Aunt Hattie promised to walk him around the block before she left for supper with her friends," he said. "I'd have to keep up with him if I let him come with us. We wouldn't be able to relax."

"And we need to relax." She sipped her drink and stared out at the ducks floating like boats in the shallows. "It's a nice evening."

Alec drank deeply from his own lemonade and stroked his scar. "Yes. I love evening time on the lake. Right when the sun begins to set it changes into this glowing yellow that changes the houses and trees. Colors everything with a soft light. Aunt Hattie calls that the pretty sun."

"It is pretty," Marla said, her smile real this time. "I like your Aunt Hattie."

"She has a good heart."

Then she asked him a question he hadn't expected. "Do you miss your mom?"

Caught off guard, Alec had to take a minute. "Yes, I do. Of course. But we weren't close when she died.

She never forgave me for joining the marines. We had words the last time we spoke." He stopped, stared out at the soft rays of whitewashed light hitting the lake. A sailboat glided by, slicing through the water in a silent stream. "I wish I could have told her how much I loved her."

Marla seemed to sense the regret on his face. "She knew, Alec. A mother always knows those things."

"How about you?" he asked, needing to shift the attention off himself because the light was too bright. "Do you miss your husband?"

It was her turn to stop and stare. At him. "Why do you ask that?"

"Because you asked me," he said, wishing he'd stayed quiet. "If I'm being too personal—"

"No, it's not that." She hesitated while Alec hated his own stupidity. "I…I need to go home, Alec."

What had he done? "Marla, I'm sorry. I shouldn't have pried into your marriage."

"No." She held up her hand. "I don't mind, really. But…my marriage was complicated. I wasn't always the best wife."

Shocked, he motioned to a bench. "Let's sit."

She followed him, her head down. When they'd settled against the still-warm rustic wooden bench, she turned to him. "My husband and I had troubles, lots of troubles."

"You don't have to talk about this," he replied, hoping they could get back to laughing and talking about mundane things. He rarely did that, but with Marla it came so easily.

"No, I should talk about this. I mean, to someone besides Preacher Sanderson and my mom."

He smiled at that. "Do I deserve such ranking?"

"I think you might," she said on a quiet, sweet note. "I trust you, Alec."

She trusted him. Alec didn't know why those words touched him so much. He knew his buddies trusted him. They talked about everything from football to their deepest fears, but they did it in man-speak, with a lot of grunts, back-slapping and teasing remarks coupled with blunt observations. But to have this interesting, pretty, quiet woman tell him that she trusted him… Alec didn't know how to respond.

"I *can* trust you, right?" she asked, fear now solid in her eyes.

"You know that already," he replied. "Or you wouldn't have said that to me."

She set down her big cup. "Okay, then. Because I need to say some things to you and I don't want you to take them the wrong way."

"About your marriage?"

"About that and about…you and me."

Alec's heart did a funny little turn. "Are you breaking up with me before we even start dating?"

"Don't you want to know about why I wasn't a good wife *before* we even start dating?"

"Are you saying you want to date me?" he teased, hoping to bring the light back into her eyes.

"Are you sure you want to date me?" she countered, serious.

"I trust you, too," he retorted in an effort to bring the conversation back to a safe level. "You must have been a good wife. You're certainly a great mother."

"I try to be a great mother," she replied, "but being a good wife is much harder."

So she didn't like being married?

Which meant she wasn't nearly ready to return to dating, let alone getting married again to anyone. Since he wasn't sure about either of those things, he at least could listen to her. As a friend and nothing more. He wanted to feel relieved, but instead he felt deflated.

"Tell me why you don't think you were a good wife, Marla. You *can* trust me."

She stared out over the water, her gaze following the mother duck and her ducklings. "I fell out of love with my husband," she finally said. "But I didn't have the courage to tell him that or to work on our marriage. I stayed because of our daughter." She turned to stare at Alec, her gaze searching him as if looking for censure or judgment. "I tried to be a good wife but he was always looking for a thrill—fast cars, fast boats, fast money. He fell in with some bad people, and they used him to plan a heist at the jewelry store he owned and managed. They robbed the store and killed him."

She stopped, put a hand to her mouth. "On the one day I was running late, Alec. The one day I'd asked him to pick up Gabby from preschool and keep her at the store. Just until I could get back there to take her home." Marla lowered her head. "I was trying to start my bakery business and he disapproved. We'd argued that morning. He didn't want to pick her up. Said it wasn't his place. He had to work but I didn't need to."

Alec watched her face, saw the horror there and understood what she'd been hiding and why. This went deeper than just being a grieving widow. He wanted to pull her close and tell her about the last conversation he'd had with his mother, about how bitter their words to each other had been, but Marla would probably push him away right now. So he just listened.

"Gabby and Charlie came back and walked in on the whole thing, but Charlie shoved her toward the co-worker who'd been alone in the store when the robbers came in. She took Gabby behind the counter and sounded the alarm, or I might have lost my daughter, too."

Alec tried to imagine how something such as this could frighten a young girl. "Did Gabby see the shooters?"

"No, thankfully not. But she saw the men and heard the salesclerk crying. They heard the shots and…she was so scared when I got there, she couldn't even speak. The police found her hiding under the desk with the shocked woman who'd been with her. Charlie distracted the robbers so the clerk could get Gabby away from them. They caught the men who did it, so I can at least breathe easy that they'll be behind bars for the rest of their lives. But I don't know if my little girl will ever be the same."

Alec's heart went into another tailspin. "And that's why she's so afraid of men?"

"Yes," Marla said. "And that's the reason I can't start dating anyone right now, including you. Especially you."

He understood a lot now. "I get why you don't want me around Gabby," he said. "But what about you? Are you afraid of me, Marla?"

Marla hadn't wanted to blurt things out to Alec in such a way, but she did trust him and she knew he was a kind, decent man who'd understand her reasons for ending things with him before they ever got started. But sitting here now, she wondered if she hadn't waited too long. Why had she encouraged him, flirted with him, hoped he'd notice her?

Because you care about him. Because he's a good friend who's helped you and made you laugh and made you feel alive again.

Was it so wrong of her to want to keep seeing Alec? Or was he right? Was she afraid to try again?

"I'm not afraid of you. That's silly. I told you, I have to protect my daughter."

He looked shocked and then resigned. "I see."

When his hand went up to his scar, Marla knew he'd misunderstood her. "Alec, it's not what you think."

"No, I understand," he said, compassion coloring his eyes. "I was around a lot of frightened children when I was in the marines. Lonely, hungry children full of fear for any American soldier. We had to be very careful with them, to get them to gain our trust. We were considered the bad guys."

"But you're not a bad guy," Marla replied. "It's just that Gabby can't distinguish who's safe and who's dangerous. She's at that age where the boogeyman can be very real."

He stood, tossed his cup into a nearby trash can and offered her a hand. "I think we need to finish our walk."

Confused, Marla stood. "Okay. But this doesn't mean we can't be friends. We can visit with each other, even go out now and then. It's just—"

"It's just that you don't want me around your child," he replied, his words cool and quiet. Or so it seemed. "I would never do anything to upset a child, Marla. You have to know that." He shrugged. "That's why I always wait until sunset to even venture out for my walks with Angus."

"It's not your physical scars," Marla said, needing him to understand. "I'm not that cruel."

"I know you're not," he replied after they crossed the bridge and rounded the curve toward the shoreline across from the Victorian house. "I wouldn't go against your wishes, either. But this puts us in a real pickle."

"I know," she said, the sound of children laughing only bringing this issue home. "And I don't know what to do."

"You said you trusted me," he reminded her. "Why don't you try trusting your own instincts?"

"My instincts tell me to be careful."

"So this isn't just about taking care of Gabby?"

Marla saw where he was headed. "You think I'm hiding behind that? That I'd use my daughter's fragility to keep myself at arm's length?"

"I don't doubt your concerns about Gabby are real, but I'm starting to think you're the one who's afraid of me."

Marla couldn't deny her fears. "I'm afraid of getting involved again, yes. It's still too soon. We're getting to know each other and that's about all I can handle right now."

Alec's face was lined in shadows of regret. "We'll have to do our best to stay friends, then. Close friends." He turned when they were behind the shelter of a towering live oak. "Friends who call each other, who trust each other, who respect each other."

"Can we do that—try to be friends?" she asked, hoping if nothing else they could make this work.

"I hope so. But sooner or later, you might get tired of

hiding me from your daughter." He didn't say it, but she could almost see what he was thinking. *And yourself.*

She didn't respond to that silent condemnation. "And sooner or later, you might get tired of not being able to meet Gabby. And maybe, tired of my hang-ups."

Alec turned to face her, his hands on her arms. "If things were different, if Gabby wasn't so scared and if I wasn't so scarred, what would be next for us?"

Not ready to face that, she looked out at the water and listened to the sound of a couple laughing as their sailboat glided by. "I don't know. I can't be sure." And then she looked up at him, her heart coming to the surface. "I'm afraid I might not ever get over my scars, either."

He backed up to stare down at her. "Then maybe Gabby's issues aren't the real problem between us. Maybe it's more about your problems and how you need to deal with them."

His words stung Marla with the intensity of a bee's bite. "You could be right. But I'll have to decide how to deal with that all on my own."

Then she saw a spark of anger in his eyes, right before he tugged her close. "Think about this while you're trying to figure things out." He leaned down and gave her a quick but gentle kiss that left her wanting more. Wanting to know him more.

"Alec…"

"Not a word," he said. "Not tonight. It's time for me to take you home. We'll talk again soon."

But she knew they were done for now. He was hurt and angry and still as scared as her little girl. So they walked back to his house and he drove her the short distance to her apartment over the shop.

"Thank you," she said. "For everything."

He nodded. "It was nice. A nice day. One I'll remember for a while to come."

Marla watched as he got back in his car and headed back to the big, lonely house and returned to the solitude that kept him so isolated. She decided that he needed to take a good long look at himself, too.

She might have problems and issues stemming from how her husband had died, but Alec was the one who was still afraid to come out of the darkness.

Chapter Ten

Alec stood on the weathered deck of AWOL, the bay-side camp house he and his three friends had bought as a getaway once they were all back stateside. The four-bedroom house with the long living/kitchen combination up front was really a glorified man cave and fishing camp, but it served another purpose for all of them. It was completely private and off the beaten path, tucked back in the dense woods where the East River met Mill-brook Bay. Here they could go hunting and fishing, grill food and swap war stories by a campfire.

Alec grinned, thinking they should just put up a big sign that stated No Girls Allowed. None of them ever brought a woman here. That was the only unwritten rule. That and the sign Preacher had put over the porch door: "And he said to them, 'Follow me and I will make you fishers of men.'"

Preacher expected the best of his buddies. He not only wanted them to catch fish and share with the masses, but he also wanted them to teach others how to function in life.

Alec was trying to abide by that rule with the

Caldwell Canines Service Dog Association. He'd put in a bid on the old car lot his overly eager Realtor had found. With a little elbow grease and some remodeling, the building would make a great kennel and training facility. So he hoped to rally his friends into helping with the renovations, to save some funding for the participants and to have some downtime doing some hard work.

Work that would make him so tired, he'd be able to sleep instead of thinking about a certain Cupcake Girl.

He heard a car pulling up underneath the massive wooden pilings that held the rickety old cottage up and served as a great covered parking area. About fifteen feet above the sand and surf to avoid flooding during the frequent storm surges brought on by hurricanes, the pilings had withstood all kinds of weather and all types of previous owners.

Alec didn't bother seeing who was down below. The old, stripped-down black Jeep was his first clue. When he heard laughter and snorts, he knew it had to be Blain and Rory. Hunter might show up late or not at all, usually on his shiny Harley, and usually with a white toy poodle tucked against his chest. Or he'd do his usual thing and sneak up on them without making a sound. The man could move through a room like an unseen shadow. Alec didn't know the full story on Hunter, but he figured if Hunter wanted to talk he would, sooner or later.

Preacher took the old steps two at a time. "How ya doing tonight, Caldwell?"

"I'll be doing fine if you brought that barbeque you promised me when you called."

"I brought the drinks," Preacher replied, holding up

some liquid refreshments. "Food is in protective custody with one of Millbrook's finest." He glanced over his shoulder with a wink.

"I'm coming," Blain called, both hands full of takeout bags. "Man, these ribs smell real good."

"Let's eat out here," Preacher suggested. "We haven't done this in a while."

"Yes," Blain replied. "A rare weekend off with fishing in the forecast and less humidity in the wind."

Alec smiled at his friends. "Where's Lawson?"

"Who knows," Blain retorted, already reaching for a sauce-covered rib. "Let's eat."

"Grace," Preacher said with a mock slap on Blain's hand.

Blain frowned and lowered his head. Alec did the same. While Preacher asked for God's love, forgiveness and continued blessings and added a special prayer for the safety for armed forces all over the world, Alec slid in his own short prayer.

Please help me to deal with my feelings for Marla in a positive, sure way, Lord.

He didn't realize Rory was done with the blessing until Blain cleared his throat. When Alec opened his eyes, both his friends were staring over at him.

"Sorry," he said, one hand scrubbing across his scar. "I had a lot to pray about."

"Talk," Blain said, passing coleslaw and baked beans as he eyed Alec.

"He's not one of your suspects," Rory reminded him with his ever-present good-natured smile. "If he doesn't want to talk about it, we can't make him." Then he withheld the box of ribs.

"Okay, all right." Alec filled his plate and held his hands together. "I think Marla and I are finished."

"Did you ever get started?" Blain asked between bites of tender smoked meat.

"We were kind of started, but we both have so much going on and, as you both know… I have a lot of excess baggage. I think I scared her."

"Scared her?" Rory asked, holding his half-eaten rib in the air. "In what way?"

"Not the way you think," Alec replied. "She's been great with my physical problems. But she's got a four-year-old daughter who was with her father when the family jewelry store was robbed, over in Tallahassee. They walked in on the robbery in progress but the little girl didn't see her father get gunned down, thanks to a sales associate shielding her. But she heard everything—guns going off and her father telling the clerk to take his daughter and run. Now she's scared of most men."

Blain dropped his rib bone and wiped his fingers on a paper towel. "I remember that case—Hamilton's Jewelry Store?"

"Marla's husband was the owner," Alec said, shaking his head. "Marla's Marvelous Desserts?"

"I can vouch for that," Preacher said between bites. "She is one marvelous cook."

Blain nodded, his dark eyes sparked with interest. "That case made all the news stations in Florida. We were alerted with an APB on the suspects. Charlie Hamilton—his family owned several stores throughout the state but after he inherited, he kind of let things go, management-wise, and lost or had to sell most of them."

Alec leaned back. "Do you have any of the details?"

Blain nodded. "Yeah, but not much more to tell now.

He fell in with some bad people who set out to rob him. He was killed at the scene and it only came out much later—after the perpetrators were behind bars—that his little girl had been with him when he returned to find the robbers with a gun on the female salesclerk. He distracted the robbers so the clerk could grab the little girl and hit the alarm. Robbers took off when they heard sirens. They caught the suspects down in Miami, probably about to board a boat for parts unknown to meet up with a fence. They took a significant amount of cash and jewels but the sales associate identified 'em. I think she moved back to the West Coast."

Preacher's frown indicated he did not like this conversation. "Has Marla talked to you about this, Alec?"

Alec set down his drink. "Yes. She wanted to explain why it's not a good idea for us to get any closer. Gabby's still got some issues with adult men. She thinks we're all boogeymen."

Blain's eyes widened. "Hey, we don't need to repeat any of this. I was telling you the facts that you could find in any old news article. Didn't mean to make matters worse."

"No, it's okay," Alec said. "Preacher, you know I wouldn't have asked if Marla hadn't already told me most of this. I'm just trying to understand. Trying to accept that Marla and I might not have any kind of future together."

"Do you want a future together?" Rory asked in his minister voice.

"I might have if not for Gabby's needs and, well, look at me. I look like the boogeyman."

Blain snorted on that one. "You're serious? Has this kid seen you? Has she run away from you?"

"She hasn't seen me yet," Alec replied, "but what if she does run away when we finally meet?"

"What did Marla say?" Rory asked.

"She said we could be friends, maybe meet for coffee or dinner, but nothing more for now."

Blain slapped him on the shoulder. "Then that's what you have to accept for now. If she's getting the girl the help she needs, her fears could go away and then she'll see you for the good-looking, great man you really are." He poked Alec with his elbow. "Hey, ugly, pass me the beans."

Preacher's blue-eyed gaze moved between them. "Ah, y'all are so sweet when you get all mushy on each other like that."

Alec smiled in spite of creating his own personal pity party. "I guess you're right," he said to Blain. "What do you think, Preacher?"

"I think…all in God's own time, boys."

"Hey, those ribs smell good."

Blain almost knocked over his drink. "Lawson, I've told you not to sneak up on me. One day I'm gonna pull my weapon on you."

Hunter Lawson's midnight blue eyes were as calm and clear as the quiet bay out beyond the sand. "I checked. Knew you'd put your weapon on the kitchen counter." He snagged a piece of Texas toast. "Probably so you wouldn't shoot yourself trying to get to those ribs."

When his little fuzzy companion trotted up behind him, the others just shook their heads. No one was going to tell Hunter Lawson that a poodle named Roxie did not fit his image. The first time they'd seen the little ball of fur, Hunter had sent all of them a glaring frown and stated, "She's not my dog."

And yet, Roxie was always with him.

"He's good," Alec said, waving Hunter to a chair. He was glad the attention had moved to Hunter and the heat was off him for now.

But maybe Blain had a point. Why should he give up on Marla? He'd always found a way to make things work in life. He'd have to figure out a way to make things work with her.

When the conversation turned to Caldwell Canines, he realized he had the perfect way to keep Marla in his life for now.

Marla's cell buzzed through her apron pocket.

"Not now," she said to the offending phone. She had to get this birthday cake done before she left today since the excited mother of a one-year-old was picking it up first thing tomorrow morning. But after checking on the layers baking in the big industrial oven, Marla took a quick minute to see if one of her parents was calling her.

But the number on her caller ID stopped her.

Alec.

She hadn't heard from him in a solid week. She knew since she'd ticked off the days in her head. Since he hadn't left a message, she almost didn't call him back. But after two hours of decorating a fire-truck-themed cake, she needed some fresh air.

"Hey, Brandy, I'm going to take a quick walk over to the park for some exercise." Figuring this return phone call wouldn't last long, she added, "Call me if you need me."

Brandy yelled, "Okay, boss" and kept right on icing cupcakes, one eye on the front counter.

Marla crossed over to the canal that eventually ran into the lake. Millbrook got its name from an old grist mill that still sat on the canal—or brook, as it was called at the turn of the past century. The old mill had been restored to showcase the town's history, but it wasn't really a working mill anymore. It just made for a lovely centerpiece in the downtown park. Marla enjoyed watching the big wheel move, its slow and steady rhythm and flowing water always soothing her when she was frazzled.

Such as right now.

Marla found a bench and sat down to listen to the water gurgling along the canal. Down the way a few people were floating along on colorful inner tubes. On the distant shore, a blue heron slowly lifted its spindly legs and searched for minnows in the shallows.

It was a nice day. Maybe she'd take Gabby for a walk later, meaning she'd walk while Gabby rode her tricycle with her favorite bear, Boo, settled in the flower-encased basket.

Should she call Alec back?

Marla debated for a full five minutes. It wouldn't hurt to talk to him—as a friend. Maybe he wanted to order some cupcakes.

Right.

She hit the number and waited, her breath hitching in a moment of panic. She was just about to hang up when the phone stopped ringing.

"Marla, hi."

He obviously had caller ID, too.

"Hi," she said, gulping a breath that almost made her cough out loud. "I...I saw you'd called."

"Hope I'm not bothering you," he said.

He sounded nervous, which only made her stomach flutter even more. "No. I'm taking a break. It's so nice out today."

"Not bad for a Monday," he replied. "Listen, I won't keep you. I was wondering if you'd still be interested in helping to raise funds for Caldwell Canines."

Marla had not expected that. Had he really just called her to get her to sign on to help with his foundation?

"Marla?"

"Yes, I'm here. Of course I still want to help."

What else could she say? This was better than not seeing him at all. But it might make things hard for her.

"Oh, good." He let out a sigh. "I was afraid you'd say no."

"I told you I wanted to do something to help," she said, reminding herself of that, too. "What's the plan?"

"Can we meet for dinner and discuss it?" he asked.

Marla closed her eyes and shot up an emergency prayer. This was for a good cause and she needed all the exposure she could get if she wanted her business to continue on a good upward swing. And, she missed Alec. Which was silly, but this way they could get to know each other a little bit more without risking anything. A fund-raising effort would involve a lot of people, so they'd have a buffer between them.

To protect her, him or both of them?

She decided both. "Dinner would be good. When?"

"How about Thursday night?"

"Thursday would work."

She'd give her parents a break and ask Brandy if she'd like to earn some extra money. Brandy loved Gabby and Gabby loved it whenever Brandy came over. They played games and read books and watched videos.

"Are you sure?" he asked. "I mean, are you sure you want to do this?"

"Absolutely," she blurted. "I believe in what you're doing, Alec. I want to help."

"I get that," he said. "But are you sure you still want to deal with me?"

Did he still think this was about his outward scars?

"Yes," she said, meaning it. "Look, this is hard for both of us. You know my reasons for taking things slow. And I understand how you're still getting used to your injuries. We can do this, Alec. We can put all of that aside to help wounded warriors who need service dogs."

Now he'd gone all silent on her.

"Alec?"

"Yes, I agree. We'll make this project a priority. I appreciate you," he said. "I'll pick you up around seven on Thursday."

And with that, he was gone.

He appreciated her, though.

Marla stared at the old oaks mushrooming out over the water and wondered if she'd have to accept appreciation when what she really wanted was…something stronger.

Chapter Eleven

"You have my number, right?"

Brandy gave Marla's frantic question a wry reply. "Uh, yes. I've had your number since I was twelve, Marla. You know we did go through school together even if you are older than me." She grinned and fluffed Marla's hair. "Will you relax? Gabby-bug and I will be just fine, won't we?"

Gabby giggled and ran to Brandy's outstretched arms. "We will, we will." She stood back and smiled up at Brandy. Then she reached one hand toward Marla. "Mommy, come dance with us."

Marla laughed and joined in. She'd texted Alec and told him to call her and she'd meet him behind her shop. A set of stairs behind the shop led up to a small deck and the back door to her kitchen. Brandy would make sure Gabby was distracted so Marla could make it out the door.

A covert operation but a necessary one.

Still laughing and dancing to one of Gabby's favorite animated songs from the movie *Frozen*, she felt the buzz of her phone against the pocket of her jeans.

"Whoa, got to go," she said, giving Brandy her cue.

"Gabby-bug, tell your mama night-night. She has to go do a good deed for someone."

"A nice man or a scary man?" Gabby asked, her dark brown eyes going wide. She dropped her hands and went still while she waited for Marla's answer.

"A nice *person*," Marla replied. "Give me a kiss for sweetness," she added, leaning down.

Gabby reached up and hugged her tight and for a minute, Marla wanted to stay right here with her little girl. But she'd have to venture out sooner or later and she'd already waited until later—way later. Maybe God was nudging her in a new direction.

"I'll be back early," she told Brandy. "Be sweet, Gabby."

"I'm always sweet," Gabby said. Then she ran back toward Marla. "I have to be a good girl."

Marla heard the trace of pain and fear in that innocent statement. "You are the very best girl I know, but you don't have to worry. Remember, we're safe here."

Gabby bobbed her head and went back to dancing.

"Let's dance in your room," Brandy suggested. She turned and danced toward the hall to the bedrooms.

Brandy ran down the hall after Gabby, their laughter sounding in Marla's ear as she hurried out the back door, locking it behind her.

Dear Lord, I hope I'm making the right decision by helping Alec. I know You'll show me the way.

She bounced down the stairs and hurried to where Alec had parked on the street behind the shop, glad that the window to Gabby's room was located on the front of the apartment.

Alec was waiting for her in a two-seater convertible.

"How many cars do you have?" she asked, out of breath from her quick getaway.

"More than I need," he admitted with a grin. "You look nice."

Marla's heart did the happy dance. Why did she feel this way with a man who was all wrong for her? A shard of guilt hit at her, making her edgy and confused. Was he wrong for her? Or did she tend to use her husband's bad habits to push away a second chance at happiness? Was she holding back on purpose, citing her own issues and her daughter's fears as her reasons?

"Just old jeans and a clean shirt," she said to downplay his compliment. Glad he was dressed casual, she felt a little better. This was more about business than fun, after all.

"I like you in old jeans and a clean shirt," he said with an amused smile. After opening her car door, he held the door and stared down on her. "It's good to see you again, Marla."

Marla nodded, shocked at how his amber eyes could make her feel. Her whole being buzzed with awareness.

When he came around and got in the car with her, she was instantly aware of the tiny space between them. This date might be about business, but her heart was definitely calling the shots with a beat of that something more she'd tried to put out of her mind.

"Are you okay?" Alec asked with a quick glance.

"Fine," she replied. "Just glad to be able to help you."

He gave her a gaze that told her he didn't believe that.

But he left it alone and soon they were zooming along in traffic. Marla hadn't even bothered to ask where he was taking her.

* * *

Alec pulled the convertible off the road and onto a gravel lane. "I thought we'd eat out at the River House."

Marla's pleased expression gave him hope that she truly did want to be with him tonight. That she was willing to help him because she wanted to, not out of some sense of guilt.

"I haven't eaten here in a while," she said after he'd parked the car underneath a moss-draped live oak. "We didn't come here often when I was a kid. My daddy thought it was overpriced."

"It is expensive, but the food's worth it," he said, wondering if her comment was a dig toward his wealth.

Marla didn't think that way, did she?

"We came on special occasions," she explained. "My birthday or their anniversary. My high school graduation."

Alec didn't mention that he and his mother used to come out here just about every Sunday after church. "I hope you enjoy it."

Marla looked down at her clothes. "Maybe I should have dressed."

"You're perfect," he said. "The food is good and the atmosphere is casual, especially on a Thursday night. Not as many tourists."

"I guess you're right," she said, her gaze sweeping over the big covered patio. "Can we eat on the porch?"

"Sure."

They were greeted by a cute hostess who gave Alec an interested smile until he turned his head. Then the young girl looked shocked but she managed to catch herself before she outright gawked at him.

"Right this way," she said, clearly trying to decide what had happened to him.

He gave Marla an apologetic gaze, wishing he could get past having a scar slashed across his face. Others had come home with deeper, more serious wounds.

Marla surprised him by hooking her arm in his and shooting him a bright smile. "It's not every night I get to have dinner with a real hero." She spoke in such a loud voice that Alec gave her a concerned stare. "I mean, a *real* hero. A soldier."

The girl glanced back at them. "Wow, that's pretty cool." Then she looked sheepish. "Thank you for serving our country."

Alec nodded and tried to ignore the interested glances coming from the other diners. "Just doing my job."

After the girl seated them at an intimate table for two out over the water, he looked over at Marla. "That wasn't necessary," he said, touched nonetheless.

She looked embarrassed. "Did I make it worse?"

Alec didn't think it could get worse. "I'm used to it but, no, you didn't do anything wrong." He wanted to reach across, take her hand and tell her that few people would be so kind. "In fact, it was pretty amazing. I believe you did what my mother and Aunt Hattie would call a bless-your-heart moment. You explained things to that poor girl in a way that didn't offend her. She probably hasn't even realized you politely put her in her place."

"My mama taught me to be tactful," Marla said. "And the girl didn't mean anything hurtful. I'm sure she's wishing she hadn't stared at you like that."

"You handled it better than I usually do," he said. "Thank you."

Marla was a good person who'd had a great tragedy in her life. Like his mother. But unlike his mother, Marla hadn't allowed bitterness to close her off from the world. Maybe that was why he was so attracted to her. She brought out the hope in people.

She stared at her menu now as if it was a really good novel. "I…I can't decide what to eat."

"Marla?"

"What?" She finally glanced over at him.

"I appreciate you."

She put down the menu. "If you keep telling me that, I might lose my appetite."

Shocked, Alec blinked. "Excuse me?"

"You appreciate me. That's great, Alec. But you've said that to me a couple of times now and if we're friends you don't need to keep saying that. Friends help other friends. That's the rule."

"I don't always go by the rules," he said, a sense of relief moving through him. She cared about him. More than she wanted to admit. "Maybe I could say something else to you?"

She picked up her menu again. "What would that be?"

He did lean in this time. Crooking his index finger over the menu, he tugged it down. "That I like you and I'm sorry about how we ended things last time we were together. That I've missed you this week and it felt like a year instead of a few days. And that I want us to work this out, somehow."

Her expression changed from stubborn and stoic to smiling and soft. "I would say I appreciate that, but…"

They both burst out laughing, causing heads to turn yet again. "We're the topic of the night, I think," Alec whispered. "We'd better order before we get kicked out of here."

"You bring that out in me," she said, shaking her head. "I become reckless when I'm with you."

"Is that a bad thing?" he asked, thinking they had not been anywhere near reckless in his mind.

"It could be," she admitted. "I think I've pushed you away because I'm afraid. But I've used every excuse I could find."

"And what about Gabby?"

Marla's expression changed again, her eyes going a misty green. "She's certainly not an excuse but I have to take this one step at a time. She misses her daddy and she's still shy and frightened around other men. I think since she's known my dad since birth, she isn't afraid of him. It's about trust. I'd have to teach her that she can trust you."

"And how do we go about doing that?"

"I don't know," Marla replied. "I'm so afraid, Alec. I can't bear to see her in pain."

"I'd never do anything to hurt her," he said, reaching for Marla's hand. "I'll follow your lead. Will that help?"

"Yes," she said, clearly relieved. "That means a lot to me."

"Good." He motioned for the attentive waitress. "Let's order, and then we really will talk about this fund-raiser. I need a good caterer and since everything you cook is *marvelous*, I'd like to hire you for the desserts at least."

"I'm pricey," she said with her usual sass back and intact.

"I'll pay whatever price," he replied, his gaze holding hers. "No matter the cost."

Alec wanted her to know this was about more than cakes and cookies. This was about his life.

And hers.

The waitress came over with a beaming smile. "Have you decided what you'd like to order?"

Alec glanced at Marla. "Ladies first."

"I'll have the shrimp and grits," she said, her mood decidedly more relaxed now. "And a house salad."

Alec ordered the catfish platter with all the trimmings. His appetite had definitely returned.

The waitress left them but they both noticed she kept grinning at them.

"A friendly girl," Alec said, more interested in talking to Marla than wondering what was up with their waitress.

By the time dessert came around, they had planned a tentative menu of all kinds of bite-size desserts. Mini-cupcakes, cookies, miniature éclairs and small tarts filled with peaches and apples.

"I can't wait to sample all of that," Alec said over coffee. They'd ordered banana pudding and it was great but he wondered if Marla could make that, too. "How do you do it?" he asked, thinking she *was* a marvel.

And clueless about it. "Do what?"

He watched the way the candlelight hit her strawberry-blond curls, making her hair shimmer like sun on water. "You're a single mother who runs her own business. Don't you get tired?"

She laughed at that. "Always. But I love what I do." She sat back and stared at her coffee. "I had just started out, working from home, when Charlie got killed. That day, I had to make dessert for a huge luncheon at the clubhouse in our neighborhood. One of my first really big jobs. I asked him to pick up Gabby from preschool and told him I'd be by for her as soon as I made my delivery." Touching her cup, she traced the gold pattern on the rim. "I stopped to explain to the staff how to serve the tiered lemon cake I'd made. I was five minutes late getting to the jewelry store. By the time I got there, the police were already there."

Alec could imagine what that scene must have looked like. "I'm sorry you had to go through that."

"Me, too. I blame myself for Gabby being there. I go over and over things in my mind, thinking if he hadn't had to go by her school he might have been there earlier and he would still be alive."

Alec saw the pain in her eyes and wished he could wipe all of this out of her memory. "Hey, you can't change any of this. Just be glad your daughter's safe."

"I am. And I'm glad his employee is okay, too. But Charlie didn't deserve to die in such a bad way."

"No, he didn't," Alec said. "But you can't blame yourself for what those criminals did that day. It's not your fault. A million things could have happened differently." He stared out over the water. "I rethink things all the time, but I can't change anything from the past. And for a while, I couldn't imagine anything in the future, either."

She smiled over at him. "I have to keep going, for Gabby's sake, and now you've found a purpose by helping others."

He nodded at that statement. "I have to keep going for the sake of all the men I watched die."

Marla put a hand to her mouth. "Here I am, going on about my woes when you've been through worse."

"Hey, I don't like to talk about what I've been through. But you make it easy to accept it."

They were sitting there smiling like goofy teenagers when the waitress brought their ticket. "I need to let you know, sir, that your bill has been paid in full."

"Really?" Alec glanced at Marla and then back to the girl.

"Who paid it?"

She waved a hand across the restaurant. "Everyone. They all offered to pay it, so we decided it's on the house. A free meal because you fought for our freedom."

Marla gave him a sweet smile. "Isn't that nice?"

Alec glanced around and everyone in the place started clapping. He was so overcome, he couldn't speak at first. "Nice, but not necessary. I don't consider myself a hero."

"Hey, accept it and be glad," Marla said.

So he did accept it with a nod and a wave. And he let out a sigh, knowing these diners had accepted him, too.

Now if he could just meet little Gabby and get her acceptance.

Chapter Twelve

"Hey, good news."

Marla smiled into the phone. "And hello to you, too, Alec. What's going on?"

"The old car dealership property—I got it. We sign the papers at the end of the month."

Marla motioned to Brandy and another worker to take over transferring a batch of I Need a Brownie Now marshmallow-pecan cream-cheese brownies to the cooling rack. The smell of baked chocolate always calmed her nerves.

While the sound of Alec's deep voice always jingled her nerves all over again. She'd need a brownie once they finished this conversation.

"That's great. So you're on your way with opening Caldwell Canines Service Dog Association."

"Yes," he said, "but we've still got a long way to go. I won't keep you, but...I was calling to see if you wanted to do something to help me celebrate."

Marla thought about her busy schedule. "I don't know. I mean, I want to celebrate with you but I have a lot of events coming up this weekend. I have to deliver a wedding cake to the church tomorrow morning and then I need to get several Mother's Day orders out, too."

"Mother's Day." She heard him exhale a breath. "I hadn't even noticed it's this coming Sunday."

"Well, we're all aware of it here. One of our busiest days. People used to cook big meals, complete with dessert. Now they order cakes and cookies and pies, anything they can find. Which gives them more time to spend with their families."

"What about you and your family?"

"I don't work on Mother's Day. We never work on Sundays unless it's an emergency and we have a backlog."

"I'll help you," he said on a quick breath. "Preacher's always telling me I need to volunteer more and he mentioned you sometimes use volunteers to help with deliveries."

Marla's heart rate bubbled over. "Uh, Alec, you're not exactly the delivery-man type."

"I won't deliver to birthday parties or crowded rooms. I don't want to scare little children."

"I didn't mean it that way," she replied. "Your smile takes away from your scar, so don't talk like that."

"Hey, I'm okay. I'm learning to laugh at myself, thanks to Preacher and others making me feel more comfortable. You included. I'll do whatever you need me to do. Ice cupcakes, test the samples, wash up all the pans."

She laughed at his animated tone. Could she get her work done with him around? Probably not. He'd be a big distraction. But they had been getting closer over the last week. Marla didn't feel any pressure with their slow-and-steady relationship. She considered Alec a friend and a business acquaintance. Having his strong presence here in her bakery? That was an entirely different matter.

"Marla, if you're not sure—"

"Okay, be here at seven sharp and wear old clothes. Be prepared to work hard. But you will be rewarded."

"I can hardly wait. You can pay me in cupcakes."

"You'll be so tired you won't be able to lift a cupcake."

"I'll be there."

She hung up with a smile on her face.

Only to turn around and find Brandy and the teenager who worked part-time grinning at her.

"Was that him?" Brandy asked with a hopeful expression.

"I don't know what you're talking about," Marla replied before going back to her busy work.

"It was him," Brandy said to Jennifer. "He's so dreamy."

"But you said he has a scar," Jennifer retorted with big eyes.

Marla shot a frown at her love-sick staff. "Hey!"

"I mean, Brandy said his scar makes him mysterious and dreamy and that he's really one of the nicest people you'll ever meet." Then she gulped air. "Am I fired?"

Marla shook her head. "Nobody is fired. I need all the help I can get. Alec is coming to help tomorrow and I expect both of you to be professional and…don't gawk at the man you call Mr. Dreamy McMarine."

"See, I told you," Brandy said, giving Jennifer a high five. "They don't know it yet, but our boss and Mr. Dreamy McMarine are gonna fall in love."

"Okay, back to work," Marla said, wagging her finger at the giggling girls hovering around her. "This is a place of business and we háve to stay busy."

That falling-in-love comment hit a little too close to Marla's tender heart. She couldn't afford to fall in love with Alec. What if Gabby never got over her fears? What then?

"Right," Brandy said with a wink. "Busy watching his every move."

She ran off to the other side of the kitchen before Marla could spread creamy icing on her pert nose.

Alec's pulse jumped and skidded in a nervous anticipation that was unfamiliar to him. He'd been a marine captain, trained to have nerves of steel. He'd commanded a large company of men during the heat of battle. What kind of man was afraid to go into a place that housed cupcakes and petits fours?

This kind of man. The kind who was slowly falling for the pretty woman in the white apron who stood behind a counter full of enticing pastries and pies.

The kind of woman he could envision in a kitchen with children running around and Angus at her feet begging for treats.

"Are you going to stand there all day or go in and help us out?"

Alec turned to find Brandy smiling at him with a pleased expression. "Uh, I guess I'll go in. I have to say, I'm a little intimidated."

She snorted in a very unladylike way. "You'll get over that soon enough. Things get mighty dicey in there at times, but at the end of the day we're all still sweet."

Alec laughed and shook his head. "Did you practice that line on some unassuming college kid?"

Brandy whirled past him and held the door open. "Sure did. Now we're engaged."

Alec liked Brandy. She was spunky and self-assured. Maybe she'd protect him from flying pans and spilled-over chocolate sauce.

"Hello," Marla called from the kitchen. "I have several people lined up to help today so let's all gather around to get our instructions."

She smiled at Alec. "We appreciate you joining us, Mr. Caldwell."

Alec waved to everyone. "My pleasure." He noticed an older gentleman giving him a crusty once-over. Alec held out his hand. "Alec Caldwell. Glad to meet you."

"Dipsey McQuire," the older man said, reaching out to shake Alec's hand. "So you're Vivian's son?"

"Yes, sir," Alec replied. The older man had a firm grip and the broad chest with pecs and biceps to back it up. "Are you the bouncer?"

Mr. McQuire let out a loud hoot of laughter. "Yeah." He pointed to Marla. "Her daddy sent me."

"Really?"

When everyone started laughing, Alec shot Marla a worried glance.

"He's messing with you," Brandy said through a giggle. "He's here to help with the heavy lifting. You get to help with that, too."

"Oh, right," Alec said, flexing his own muscles.

"I work out at the senior citizen fitness room three times a week," Mr. McQuire said. "We let young'uns in if you wanna go at it, son."

"I'll consider that, thank you," Alec replied, his eyes now on Marla. He had a feeling he'd be outdone in that fitness room.

"Mr. McQuire is retired navy." She sent him a soft smile and then shooed everyone to work. When they were alone, she walked over to Alec. "Ready for this?"

"Reporting for duty, as requested, yes."

"I run a tight ship," she replied in a mock-stern voice.

"I'm not a sailor, ma'am. Just a poor retired marine."

"You're not poor and I've always heard, once a marine, always a marine."

"I think I've met my match with your merry band of followers."

She gave him that mysterious smile again. "If you survive this day with us, you just might be a keeper."

He leaned close, the scent of her floral perfume mixing with the scent of chocolate chip cookies. Lowering his voice, he said, "I like the sound of that."

Marla's eyes flared in shades of blue-green but she slapped at his arm. "The cupcakes have eyes, you know."

He shook his head. "I guess I'd better keep my distance. Don't want to get fired right off the bat. Or whipped over by Mr. McQuire."

"I think you're safe. He talks big but I have it on good authority that he suffers gout now and then."

With that, she went back to ordering people around and Alec's respect for her went up a couple more notches.

By the end of the day, he was exhausted, amazed and pretty sure he never wanted to see another cookie or cupcake. Ever.

"I've been in a lot of tricky situations," he said to Marla as they finished tidying up, "but this day takes the cake."

"Your jokes are endearing," she said with a smirk.

He looked outside, the sound of thunder and lightning shaking the building. "At least I didn't leave the cake out in the rain."

She started giggling like a schoolgirl. "Do I need to call Mr. McQuire back here to straighten you out?"

"Please don't. I had to witness him doing a one-armed push-up at just about every stop."

"Did he make you do them, too?"

Alec bobbed his head. "Yes, but he beat me every time."

"Did you let him win?"

"Of course. I'm not completely stupid."

"Brandy said you did a great job, helping to carry the cake into the church. That's the hardest part of our job."

"It was a small cake and I followed Dipsey's instructions to the letter."

"He and my dad take turns helping out. Dad had another commitment this weekend."

"Oh, something important?"

"Yes. A deep-sea fishing trip out in the gulf."

"In this weather?"

She looked out the window. "Well, it wasn't raining this morning. Hopefully, they've made it in by now."

Alec checked his phone's weather app. The storm hovered out over the warm waters of the Gulf of Mexico. He didn't say anything to Marla since he didn't want to worry her.

"Need to go?" she asked, her gaze hitting on his phone.

"No, nothing planned tonight. What about you?"

"I'll go and pick up Gabby, and I guess I'll either

have dinner with my folks or come home and order a pizza for the two of us before I tuck her in."

Alec leaned back against a counter. "I wish I could share a pizza with you and Gabby. We never had our official celebration."

"I know," she said. "And I'd still like to celebrate your purchase of the property to build your training school." Glancing around the neat bakery kitchen to make sure they were alone, she turned back to Alec. "Her therapy is going pretty good. I'm supposed to take her for a walk around the neighborhood and encourage her to wave to anyone she sees, especially all the other grandfatherly types."

"That should make her more comfortable with strangers."

"She's afraid of Mr. McQuire but she did notice that he looks like Santa Claus."

"Is she afraid of Santa?"

Marla nodded. "That's been an issue, but I've never been one for forcing children to sit on Santa's lap just to get a picture."

"Good point."

The conversation tapered off as he watched Marla going around to check doors and set the alarm.

He walked her to the back door. "Do you have an umbrella?"

She motioned to a coatrack. "Yes. I'll be fine."

"And you'll drive carefully out to the retirement center?"

"Yes, I will."

Then he had an idea. "Have you ever considered a service dog for Gabby?"

"What do you mean?"

"Maybe if she had a dog of her own, she'd feel safer?" He brushed at the shining aluminum counter. "It could be a puppy or a smaller dog so she won't be overwhelmed. I can research different breeds, talk to some experts."

"I've never thought of that," Marla replied. "I'll ask her therapist, but I don't know that we could keep a dog, with my hours and this tiny apartment."

"Service dogs are trained to be docile when needed. And the dog could stay with your parents a lot anyway, right?"

"Yes. Gabby practically lives with them as it is."

Seeing the regret in her eyes, he reached out a hand to touch a cluster of wild curls dangling near her left temple. "You're a good mother, with good parents to help."

"I know. I just miss her when I have long days such as this one." She shrugged, her struggle evident in her eyes. "But I love what I do and I've worked hard to be independent."

"Gabby might not understand that now but one day, she'll tell you how proud she is of you. You're a great example for your daughter."

"Thanks," she replied, a soft smile pushing at the traces of fatigue on her face. "I need to spend more time with her while she's still young."

He moved his hand from her hair to her cheek. "You'll see her soon."

She touched a hand to his. "Alec, I want you to meet her. I really do. But I'm so afraid."

"I understand."

They stood there for a split second, a second between their two worlds that could define the future. When a clap of thunder hit outside the door, they took one look at each other. Then Alec pulled her into his arms and kissed her.

Marla tasted as sweet as this bakery smelled. She was all sweetness and light, all richness and temptation. She molded into his arms as if God had made her just for him. The kiss lasted through a couple more sighs and thunderclaps and then she pulled away.

"Wow, that was some reward," he said against her spice-scented hair.

Marla looked flushed and surprised. "Yes. I was going to go home and settle for pizza and ice cream… but…wow."

"Wanna try it again?"

She answered him with another kiss.

And then, they laughed and ran out into the rain together.

Chapter Thirteen

Marla breathed a sigh of relief when she finally made it out to the Millbrook Lake Retirement Village. The rain was pouring in a steady pounding of thunder and lightning and flooded roads. Her old van was pretty sturdy, but she was shaking by the time she pulled into her parents' driveway and ran up onto the tiny porch.

Her mother opened the door. "Hurry in, honey."

Marla noticed right away that something was wrong. "Mom, is Gabby okay?"

Her mom whirled and pressed a shaky finger to her lips. "She's fine. She's in the den coloring a picture for you."

"What is it, then?" Marla asked, worry spiking through her system. Then her heart skidded in realization. "Where's dad?"

"Honey, he hasn't checked in. The charter boat hasn't returned to the marina."

"What?" Marla went still but from the look on her mother's face, she recovered and went into action. "Mom, it's going to be all right. I'm sure they're safe.

The boat captain is experienced, and even if they're out in this storm his crew will know what to do."

"I know, but I'm so worried."

Marla refused to think past the obvious. "Has the Coast Guard been alerted?"

"Yes." Mom held her hand to her chest. "I'm staying near the phone but I don't want to upset Gabby."

"No, we can't do that." Marla guided her mother back toward the den and kitchen area. "We'll make grilled cheese sandwiches and…act natural. It won't be long until her bedtime so we just have to occupy her for a couple of hours."

Joyce hugged Marla tight. "You are so strong, honey. I'm so glad you're here."

Marla thought she wasn't that strong. The memory of Alec's kisses just a short while ago gave her the strength she needed right now, however.

That and a prayer held on a breath she wasn't quite able to let go.

Alec stood in his office, watching the rain through the yellow glow of the security lights surrounding his home. He was worried about Marla's dad but he hadn't called her yet. He didn't want to upset her if Mr. Reynolds hadn't made it home yet. But darkness had settled over the lake quickly with this gloomy sky. He'd give it another half hour. Then he would call her.

"It's bad out there," Aunt Hattie said from the doorway. "I thought you might like some coffee."

Alec turned and rushed to help her with the tray she carried with coffee and a sandwich.

"I know you said you weren't hungry but you need

to eat something. I baked a big roast for Sunday dinner but I'd say a roast beef sandwich might be in order for tonight."

"Thank you," he said, taking the tray and setting it on a nearby table, where they always shared these intimate meals. His aunt made sure he was well fed. "Where's your dinner?"

"I had a bite when I was slicing the roast," she said with a shrug. "I did bring my one cup of decaf." She lifted her dainty cup off the tray and took a seat across from where Alec stood.

He sat down and admired the hefty sandwich. "Why is it that food is so important, Aunt Hattie?"

"Well, we have to eat to stay alive," she said on a laugh. "Is there more to it? Yes, of course. Food brings people together and gives us comfort."

"I remember mother's funeral," Alec said, wondering why he needed to talk about this. "All that wonderful food. I wasn't even hungry but each time I'd turn around, someone would hand me a plate of good Southern cooking."

"It's a tradition," his aunt said, her hand holding her cup close. "We really don't know what to say or do in times of great grief. But food speaks for us. We cook and we bring food and try to keep the kitchen running, and then we stand around and we hope."

Alec took a couple of bites of the sandwich, the warm tender beef covered with spicy gravy giving him the exact kind of comfort his aunt explained. On a rainy night such as this, a warm sandwich and a sweet aunt for company was more than he deserved.

He didn't deserve Marla's kisses, either, but that kind of comfort sure was hard to refuse.

"Is there a reason for this discussion?" Aunt Hattie asked in her quiet, kind way.

He put down the fat sandwich and wiped his hands on a pale blue linen napkin. "Marla Hamilton," he said. "She's amazing. She brings people comfort and happiness and she makes these impressive concoctions that… might not be good for our health or our waistlines, but they seem to be a necessary part of life."

"I've never seen anyone but maybe a supermodel frown at a cupcake," his aunt retorted. She patted her midsection. "Obviously I've had my fair share."

"I did, too, today."

"So you enjoyed helping Marla?"

"I did. It's hard work but I had a good time. I'm exhausted but proud of myself. I was actually the jumper a few times."

Aunt Hattie quirked one manicured eyebrow up into a question mark. "The jumper? You didn't have to use a parachute to deliver cookies, did you?"

Alec laughed and shook his head. "No, nothing so dangerous as that. The jumper is the one who gets out of the delivery van and actually hand-delivers the items. I didn't really jump, however. I had to be very careful with some of the items." He nibbled his sandwich again. "We took a wedding cake to the church this morning."

"Oh, yes. I heard the Horton girl was marrying the Baker boy. They'll make a good match."

Alec laughed at his aunt's report. It was close enough. If he pressed for details on that analysis, his aunt would give him a thorough rundown of the family tree on both sides.

"That's right," he said. "Cute couple. A small cake, white with silver eatable pearls and delicate cream lace icing."

"I'm impressed, Chef Caldwell."

"Marla's young assistant, Brandy, aka the Drill Sergeant, explained each delivery to me in meticulous detail. In case the customer had any questions or complaints." He took a sip of his coffee. "Although I think she just enjoys describing Marla's work to everyone. A good word-of-mouth salesperson."

Aunt Hattie nodded in approval. "Marla has a good head on her shoulders, and she's worked hard to grow her business and help downtown Millbrook come back to life. The report at the last chamber of commerce meeting showed we've been attracting more and more tourists to our little inland hamlet. I give part of that credit to Marla's Marvelous Desserts."

"Everyone loves cupcakes," Alec said, reaffirming their earlier discussion.

They laughed and moved on to other subjects. Alec glanced at his empty plate. "Thank you for the food. It did bring me comfort."

Aunt Hattie stood, but he got up, too. "I'll take this to the kitchen, and then I'm going to call Marla."

Aunt Hattie inclined her head to one side. "Oh, so you two have really hit it off?"

"We're good friends. But I need to call her to check on her father. He went out on a deep-sea-fishing charter today and…well, the storm moved in and she was worried about him."

"Let me take the tray, then," Aunt Hattie said. "You stay here and call Marla. And let me know that everything is okay."

Alec didn't argue with her. Giving her a kiss on the cheek, he leaned close. "Thank you. You are my favorite aunt."

"I know," she said with a grin.

He watched her go, wondering how two sisters could be so completely different. His mother loved him but she never was the motherly type. He missed her anyway.

Opening his phone, he hit Marla's number and waited for her to pick up. He hoped she'd have good news regarding her father's whereabouts.

Marla's cellphone buzzed in her pocket. Glancing toward where her mom sat reading to Gabby, she turned away. Alec's number and name flashed across her phone screen.

"Hello?" she said on a low breath.

"Hey. I…I'm just calling to check on your dad."

"He's not home yet," she said. "We can't leave or make any calls. Gabby is still up. So we're just waiting to hear."

"I can make a few calls for you," he said, his deep voice calm and sure. "They might be waiting it out or they could be near the marina. Sometimes it's hard to connect when you're away from shore."

"Thank you," Marla replied. "I'd appreciate anything you can find out."

She ended the call and turned to her mom with a smile. "That was my friend who helped me today, Mom. He's going to call around about that concern we have."

"Oh, what a good idea," her mom said with misty-eyed clarity. "Your friend is very considerate."

Gabby, always watchful, looked up at Marla. "When is Pawpaw coming home to tuck me in?"

"I don't know, sugar-pea," Marla said. "But Memaw and I will tuck you in."

"Am I staying here tonight, Mommy?"

"Since it's raining so much, we're both staying here. A special time with Memaw."

Gabby clapped her hands. "Yay. Are you sleeping in my room?"

"Yes," Marla replied in an animated voice. "On the other bed that matches yours."

"Can we go to bed now?"

"I can certainly get you ready and then, after we read and tuck you in, maybe I'll stay up with Memaw a while, okay?"

"'Kay," Gabby replied. She hopped up and turned to her grandmother. "I'll come get you when I'm weady, Memaw."

"Okay, sweetie," Mom said, her words hiding the fear in her low voice. She nodded to Marla. "Go on. I'll check on some things myself."

Alec closed his phone after rallying his buddies together. Blain Kent was calling around to check on any reports of charter boats not reporting in or making it back to shore. Hunter Lawson was down at the marina, doing his thing by questioning and intimidating anyone who'd listen to him.

And Preacher was tuned in to his hotline to God. He was praying and he'd told Alec he'd get the church prayer chain on this, too.

Since they had two friends in the Coast Guard who'd also promised to do some checking, Alec felt they had done everything they could do for now. But

Alec couldn't stop the restless need to do something constructive.

"Aunt Hattie, I'm going down to the marina."

His aunt stuck her head around the sitting room door. "Is there news?"

"No, but I can't sit here waiting. I'll go down and meet up with Hunter. See what he's heard."

His aunt inclined her head in approval. "Be careful and call me, please. I'm sending prayers."

"Thanks." Alec headed for the garage, then turned and came back to give his aunt a kiss. "You know I love you, right?"

"Or course," she said with a soft smile. "Unspoken but obvious."

"I need to tell you that more," Alec said, meaning it.

Maybe if he and his mother had said those words more to each other, she wouldn't have died angry and disappointed in him.

Marla's phone buzzed around midnight.

"It's Alec," she said to her mom.

Mom sat up and blinked. "News? Does he have news?"

They'd both sat on the couch, trying to sleep. Her mother had just dozed off.

"Alec, what have you heard?"

"Your father is fine," he said.

Marla started crying, but Mom gasped. "He's okay, Mom. It's okay."

Her mother grabbed a nearby tissue box and started wiping her eyes. "Oh, thank You, Lord."

Marla turned back to her phone. "What happened?"

"They did get caught in the storm but they managed to hold the boat steady. It was apparently a long, treacherous ride to shore. I'll let your dad tell the rest."

"Is he really okay? Are they all okay?"

"Yes. Just some bumps and bruises. I think he might have sprained a wrist when he slipped on the wet deck. I'll have him home soon."

Marla glanced out at the pouring rain. "You're bringing him home. In this weather?"

"I offered to take him to my house 'til morning but he refused. Said he could drive himself home."

"No, he can't do that. I'll come and get him."

"You will not do that," Alec said in what she could only call his marine voice. "I'm bringing him home."

"Okay," Marla replied, too tired and relieved to argue. "Thank you, Alec."

When she turned around, her mother rushed into her arms to give her a hug. "I was so scared."

"Me, too," Marla said. "But Dad's okay. They're all battered and bruised but no major injuries and…they all made it home."

Her mom stood back and wiped her eyes. "So if I heard right, Alec is bringing him home?"

"Yes, he insisted."

Marla didn't want to think about the implications of having Alec here again. While her mother went to work on making coffee and finding something for the men to eat, Marla hurried down the hallway toward Gabby's room. She'd make sure the door was pulled shut before Alec came in the house. Things had gone okay last time he was here but with this much excitement, Gabby could wake up and come running.

After giving her sleeping daughter a kiss and pulling the seashell-patterned quilt over her, Marla hurried back to the kitchen to help her mother.

She owed Alec a lot for what he'd done tonight.

He truly was the kind of man any woman could call a hero.

Chapter Fourteen

A while later, Marla heard a car pulling up into the narrow drive in front of her parents' house. "I think they're here, Mom."

Her mother headed to the front door while Marla double-checked the door to Gabby's room. Her daughter was used to sleeping in noisy houses, but Marla couldn't risk Gabby waking up tonight and seeing a man she didn't know standing in her grandparents' home.

When she peeked in, Gabby was curled up with her favorite worn bunny rabbit, her eyes closed in a peaceful slumber. Marla closed the door and let out a long sigh.

When she walked back toward the living room, her mom and dad were hugging each other tight. Mom wiped at her eyes and kept patting his shoulder. "Are you sure you're all right?

"I'm okay, honey," Dad said. "We're all okay."

Alec glanced from them to Marla. Without waiting for him to say anything, she rushed into his arms. "Thank you so much."

"Shhh," he said. "I didn't do that much. I'm just glad everyone is alive and accounted for."

Marla stood back, her pulse jumping around in an erratic nervousness. "It's been a long night. We were so worried." She went over and hugged her dad, too.

Her mom held Dad's arm. "Now, sit down right there in your chair. Alec, find a seat. We have sandwiches and coffee."

Dad let out a chuckle. "I never thought I'd actually enjoy you forcing me to sit down, Joyce. But it's such a lovely, bossy sound. I love you."

Mom got teary-eyed again. "I love you, too, silly. Don't scare me like that again, you hear?"

"I sure do. Now bring on the pampering." Dad winked at Marla. "I'll milk this for all it's worth."

Alec chuckled. "See, I told you he's fine." Then he glanced toward Marla's mom. "Thank you for the offer of food and coffee, Mrs. Reynolds, but I probably should get going. It's bad out there and the roads are flooded in places."

"Took us twice as long to get home," Dad pointed out, nursing his swollen right arm. "I haven't seen rain like this in a long time."

Marla wanted Alec to stay but she couldn't bring herself to tell him that. Mom took care of that problem.

"Alec, sit down. You can't leave without letting us at least feed you."

"Mom, it's past midnight," Marla said, giving Alec an apologetic smile and a way out if he wanted one. "He might want to go home and get some sleep."

"Oh, I'm sorry," Mom said, putting a hand to her mouth. "I didn't think about how late it is."

Alec's gaze moved from Mom to Marla, clear regret marking his features. "It is late. You all need to get some sleep, too."

He turned for the door while Marla's teeth pressed against her bottom lip. "Alec, wait," she said, the imprint of trying to keep him here burning against her skin. "One cup of coffee and then you can go."

He held the doorknob, his head down. "Are you sure about that?"

Marla swallowed back her fears. "Of course I'm sure. You helped rescue my father and his friends tonight. I won't forget that."

He turned then and gave her a grudging smile. "If you tell me you're grateful, I just might turn around and leave."

"Just come and sit down," Marla said, whirling to head toward the kitchen. She didn't miss the glance that passed between her bewildered parents. She was pretty sure she'd have some explaining to do later.

"Your dad will need to have that wrist checked again," Alec told Marla an hour later. "Preacher talked to the paramedics and promised them your dad would follow through."

"Preacher?" Marla lifted up from her spot by him on the couch. Lowering her voice since her parents had gone to bed, she stared over at Alec. "Preacher Sanderson was there tonight?"

"He's one of the first people I called. We're all on what's called a 'Good Samaritan' vessel list. We're trained to help and assist in maritime search-and-rescue."

"So you were prepared."

"We're prepared to help the Coast Guard as needed. In this case, we alerted them that I knew one of the passengers. We asked permission to help."

Her eyes flashed a sea-green. "Because you thought the worst?"

"No," Alec said. "Because Rory and I are good friends and because he's good at staying calm in a crisis and he knows the waters of the bay and the gulf better than anyone. And we both know the rules of assisting."

She sank back against the sofa pillows. "I didn't realize you two were that close. I guess there's a lot about you I don't know."

She had him there. Alec wasn't one to talk a lot about the past, or the present, either, for that matter. "Well, you know he served as a chaplain in the army, right?"

"Yes, he's talked about that some in his sermons. Did you know him back then?"

"Yes and no. We met at the pizza house here in Millbrook, between deployments. That's how I got to know Blain Kent, too."

"He's a detective," she said, nodding. "Not that Millbrook needs a lot of detectives. I've seen him doing every job available at big events—directing traffic, breaking up scuffles, helping little ladies across the street."

"Blain's a good guy. He believes in finding the truth, no matter what."

Marla did a neck roll and relaxed back against the couch. "I'm glad you have good friends who've been through the same experiences as you. Pretty cool that you all came back here."

He didn't mention Hunter. The Okie liked his privacy. And Alec didn't really want to talk about his friends. He'd rather talk about being with Marla.

And he was willing to break all the rules for that. "I'll have to take you fishing out at our camp house on the bay. It's not really a feminine place, but as long as you don't reorganize the kitchen, we should be safe."

"I'd love that," she said with a smile. Then she looked down at her hands. "I used to love fishing with my dad out on our farm. There was a small pond not far from our house."

Alec noticed she didn't mention much about her husband. So he didn't ask. "We'll make it a date, then. Maybe later in the summer."

"Yes, maybe. If my mom ever lets any of us go fishing again."

They sat there in silence for a moment. Then she asked, "So how bad was it out there on the water? I mean, how close were my dad and his friends to never coming back?"

Alec knew there were some things about which you just didn't go into detail. But he also knew Marla could handle the truth. "It was rough. The Coast Guard got the distress call right before the storm hit. The boat's engines were in distress and a storm was approaching."

He gave her direct glance. "When I left you this afternoon, I turned on my weather radio and followed the storm data. The Coast Guard started out right after receiving the call but I'd been keeping a close eye on the weather all night. When we radioed our assistance, they had already searched the perimeters of the area where the first distress signal had occurred. At first, they couldn't find any charter boats or lifeboats. Nothing."

"How did *you* find them, Alec?"

He smiled and took her hand. "I have a go-fast boat."

"You took a speedboat out in that storm?"

"Not exactly," he said. "We went around the storm."

"Okay. Why didn't the Coast Guard do that?"

"They can get through just about any water but…
the charter boat stopped responding to radio contact,
and in the dark with no radio contact, it's hard, even
for someone trained." He spread his hands wide. "The
ocean is constantly changing, so it's like searching for
pinpoints on a quilt."

She let out a gasp. "The charter boat was lost?"

Alec touched a hand to her hair. "Just couldn't be
located at first."

"There's a difference?"

"Depends on which way the wind's blowing, the drift
trajectory and several other variables. Sometimes, in
heavy weather, things get crazy out there. Once he'd
sent out the distress signal and lost contact, the captain
had to concentrate on saving everyone on board." Alec
held his hand on her shoulder. "With a power boat that
was able to skirt the waves and go around the center of
the storm, we managed to search the coordinates. We
stayed in radio contact with the Coast Guard and gave
them updates on our location."

"And you saw the charter boat?"

"We saw a flare."

She closed her eyes. "I can't tell my mother how bad
this actually became. She'll never let my dad go out in
a boat again."

Alec gave her a reassuring smile. "He'll tell her,
eventually. When we found them, they were all calm but
very aware of how dangerous things had become. With
that chop, it was hard to get to them." He shrugged.
"The Coast Guard came along right after we did. Blain
radioed them as soon as we spotted the boat and accounted for everyone. They got all the passengers off
the boat, but at least we were there to help if needed."

The fear in her eyes crushed Alec, but he wanted to be honest with her. "When we first met, you said you were afraid I was a thrill seeker like your husband. But I'm no such thing. I just—"

"Go into a storm…or you go around the storm?"

"I go where I'm needed," he replied, his hand moving through her hair. "And tonight, you needed me."

"I believe that," she said, leaning close. "What if I need you again, just to be here, to talk to me and laugh with me and cry with me? What then?"

Alec wanted to kiss her but he wasn't sure how to handle that feeling of not being able to breathe, of not being in control. He wasn't sure how to handle anything about being with Marla. "I'd want you to be very sure before you make that kind of decision. Don't mistake our mutual gratitude for each other as something else."

Surprise darkened her eyes. "Why? Because you don't want to be needed? Or are you just afraid of letting *me* get too close?"

"Isn't that what we're both feeling here? We can't get too close because of so many things."

"Such as my little girl and your scars and memories?"

Alec wanted her to need him but he was afraid to admit how much he really needed her. "I don't want you to be caught up in something you might not be ready for, Marla."

She gazed up at him, her eyes earnest and unyielding. "Shouldn't I be the one to make that decision?"

"Yes," he said, his hands pulling through her hair. "But you've been through a lot and you've made it clear you don't need any more drama in your life. I won't put you through anything else."

Her expression shifted into a frown. "You've been nothing but kind to me, Alec. Or is that it? Is this about doing the right thing and being kind? *Is* this about gratitude and friendship and nothing more?"

"It's about all of those things and more," Alec replied, pulling her toward him, needing her close to him. "We have a lot between us, but I'm willing to bridge that distance. I don't want you to be hurt. I sure don't want you to feel obligated to me because I helped find your dad."

"You made it through a lot of storms," she said, her fingers tracing his scar. "If you're worried about my doubts, don't be, okay? I'm working on the trust thing… and I'm also learning to open up to people. I pushed you away because of my own fears. I shouldn't have used my daughter's situation against you."

"I am worried," Alec said, wishing he could explain what his heart was telling him. "I'm scared to death. I've never been this close to a woman before. Not like this."

"I'm afraid, too," she admitted. "I have so many things going on in my life right now." Her fingers warmed his skin, mended his pain. "I don't want to let you go, but you're right. I need to be sure. So I can't ask you to wait."

"We don't have to rush," Alec said. "I'm not going anywhere and I hope you're not, either."

They were a breath away from each other now. "So you don't mind taking things slow?"

Alec laughed against her skin and then touched his nose to her neck. "It's like what we did tonight to help find that missing charter boat. I'll find a calm wind and travel around the long way. But eventually, I will find you, Marla."

"So I'm not lost?"

"No, you're just not in a place where I can locate you yet. You'll be okay, though. And we'll both know when the time is right."

She held her hand there on his scar. "And when we do, will you come and get me in that go-fast boat of yours?"

"Absolutely," he said before he lowered his head to hers. "I'll come straight through a storm for you."

The kiss was sweet and tender, with no hurries. Alec tugged her close, one arm wrapping around her shoulder. When he held Marla like this, he forgot his imperfections. She made him feel whole again.

He lifted away long enough to smile at her before he kissed her again, but a sound from the hallway brought them both out of the embrace.

And then a little cry pierced the night and Marla pulled away with a shocked glance toward the open bedroom door. "Oh, no."

Alec realized too late that little Gabby was standing there, screaming at him. "Let go of my mommy. Please let go of my mommy!"

Marla was off the couch and down on her knees in front of her little girl. "It's okay, baby. It's okay. This is a nice man. A good man. Gabby, okay?"

"No, no!" Gabby burst into tears again, her big eyes on Alec. "No, bad man. No!"

Alec got up and stood in a corner, his heart breaking as he listened to Gabby's wailing sobs.

And the soft sobs of the woman he'd just kissed.

Without a word, he turned and hurried out into the storm.

Chapter Fifteen

"Honey, you can't keep doing this."

Marla glanced up from looking blankly at her toast to find her mother standing there staring at her. She hated seeing the worry in her mom's eyes. "Doing what, Mom?"

"Keeping people at arm's length because you're still grieving."

Marla's appetite disappeared. It was raining again this morning, but it was a soft, cozy drizzle and the roads were passable according to the weather report. "I have to get to home," she said. "I know it's Sunday, but I have tons of paperwork to get done."

"So you don't want to spend Mother's Day with your family?"

Marla put a hand to her mouth. "Oh, I'm so sorry, Mom. I totally forgot after everything that happened last night. I'm just so worried about Gabby."

"Let her sleep," Mom said, automatically pouring Marla another cup of coffee. "She'll be fine here with Dad while you and I go to church. We can go to the chapel here on the property since the weather is still so bad."

"Dad will want to be there since it's Mother's Day."

"He gave me the best present last night," Mom said. "He survived."

Marla lifted up a prayer for that. "Yes, thankfully."

"It was nice of Alec to help," Mom said. "I'm so sorry Gabby got upset."

"It's okay," Marla said. "I know you think I'm being unreasonable about this, but…how am I supposed to let any man into my life when my child is so terrified?"

"Honey, you're the best mom I know, but Gabby will be fine. You're taking all the steps the therapist has suggested and she's improving every day. I like Alec and he seems to care about you. Give him a chance."

"I tried to do that last night," Marla admitted. "But he left when Gabby woke up. I could see the hurt in his eyes, but what can I do? I have to think of Gabby's hurt." She toyed with her napkin. "I thought I could do both—keep Gabby safe and keep Alec close. But it's not working. I can't spend time with him when my daughter needs my attention."

"You have Dad and me to help."

"Yes, and I'm blessed for that. But I take way too much advantage of both of you."

"Don't be silly," Mom said. "We're retired and we love our grandchild. It's a privilege to help out. Gabby loves it out here, and Dad knows how to handle her." She leaned across the counter. "We didn't get to talk to you about this yesterday, but Gabby's been doing better with our friends."

"What do you mean?" Marla asked, dropping the

frayed paper napkin. Her parents knew how she felt about exposing Gabby to men who scared her.

"She waved to Dipsey yesterday when he got home. She was riding her trike out front, me walking behind her. Saw him get out of his truck." Mom shrugged. "She turned to look at me, and I remained calm and told her that was our good friend Dipsey. I told her he wouldn't hurt her because he cares about Pawpaw and me and so he wants to get to know her."

Marla's heart constricted with fear. "And she didn't cry or try to hide?"

"No. She asked me if he was Santa Claus."

"But she's scared of Santa, too," Marla reminded her mom.

"We've been showing her pictures of Santa and reading her books about him," Mom explained. "And we're teaching her all about Christ and showing her pictures of Him sitting with the little children."

Marla didn't want to pick a fight with her mom this morning, but she resented her parents going behind her back to try to help Gabby. But it was really sweet of Mom to read Bible stories to Gabby. "Wow, you two have been busy."

Mom didn't even blink at the censure in her voice. "Yes, we have. We've talked to her about our friends here, about how they are safe and they want to help us love her and take care of her."

Marla wanted to be angry at her parents but the relief she felt at this bit of good news overtook her anger. "Do you think I'm being too protective?"

Her mom put a hand over hers. "I think you're trying to do the right thing. But being cautious can backfire. Do you want her to grow up filled with anxiety and fear?"

"Of course not," Marla said. "I want her to get well, to run and play and laugh and not scream in fear when she sees a man she doesn't know."

"We need to show her somehow that Alec isn't a bad guy."

Marla nodded. "I agree with that. He's suggested a puppy, maybe a service dog to help make her feel safe. He says service dogs can be trained to recognize anxiety and to calm children, even autistic children. Do you think it's possible for Gabby? Should I try that?"

"A dog might work," Mom said. "We're allowed to have small dogs here, so she could bring him out here with her. That could help her get past all of our over-bearing but well-meaning friends." She lowered her head and gave Marla a smile that held so many unspoken things. "And a puppy would distract her—and probably distract us from being so cautious and careful."

Marla hadn't thought about what her parents must go through each time they had Gabby with them. "I guess I haven't made things easy for anyone."

"Honey, this isn't about being easy. It's about being strong and doing what's right for Gabby and yourself. We'll abide by whatever you see fit, but she's growing up and, sooner or later, keeping her hidden here with us will become unrealistic."

"I don't know," Marla said. "I'll try to talk to Alec about the puppy but it might confuse her even more."

"Or it might confuse you even more," Mom said with an understanding smile. "Do you care about Alec?"

"I like him," Marla admitted. "He's a good man. He's a veteran who served his country and he almost died when he was wounded. He's trying to do a lot for Millbrook and he's got this amazing humility that I love."

She stopped, pushed away from the kitchen island. "But there's just so much between us."

"You deserve a second chance," Mom said. "You can be happy again."

"I am happy," Marla said. "I have a strong client base now and word is spreading. We're booked up through the Fourth of July." She laughed and pushed at her hair. "I'm making all of the desserts for the big fund-raiser Alec is planning for the Caldwell Canines Service Dog Association." Glancing at the calendar Mom kept on the pantry door, she said, "That's in a few weeks."

Mom lifted up and put her hands together. "That's great. You are moving up in the world." Her smile widened. "And that means you'll be working closely with Alec."

"Yes, I guess I will." Marla laughed at her mom's expressive eyes. She didn't have the heart to tell Mom that things with Alec might have to go back to a professional level. "Thanks, Mom. For the coffee and the pep talk."

Mom came around the counter. "Now, will you go to church with me?"

"Yes," Marla said. "But Gabby will want to go, too. We made cupcakes and they're still in my van along with your gift. I'll get her up and we'll have fun celebrating Mother's Day."

"Don't forget me," Dad said as he ambled up the hall carrying a potted plant. "Hid this in the back of my closet."

Mom laughed. "I know. I found it when I was putting up your shirts. I gave it some water."

"I never could surprise your mother," Dad said. He

kissed Mom and winked at Marla. "You know something? I like Alec."

"I don't doubt that," Mom said. "He helped rescue you."

"Helped me out of the boat and right onto the Coast Guard boat," Dad said. "Then followed us to the marina in that fancy boat of his. Might want to take a ride with him one day."

"Not so fast," Mom said. "Let me get over your deep-sea fishing excursion first."

Marla left her parents hugging and teasing each other.

She could have that again one day. Or maybe she could have that kind of affectionate relationship for the first time.

If she got a second chance.

"Well, hello there."

Alec shook Preacher's hand and waited for Aunt Hattie to get a good hug from Rory Sanderson. She loved all of his friends as if they belonged to her, too. Coming to church was an extra joy for her, since she approved of Rory's sermons.

"So good to see you today," Rory said to Aunt Hattie. "Hope you have a great day."

Preacher was always careful of how he handled Mother's Day Sunday with some of the females of the congregation. Aunt Hattie hadn't been able to have children of her own so she'd spoiled Alec and her nieces and nephews on her husband's side of the family.

"I shall," she said with a prim grin. "My handsome nephew is taking me out for lunch."

"Oh, really?" Preacher gave Alec a fist bump. "Let me guess, the Back Bay Pizza House?"

"I'll eat pizza," Aunt Hattie countered with a gleam in her eyes. "Want to join us?"

Rory burst out laughing. "Thank you, but I'll be enjoying lunch with my own mom up over in Crestview."

"That's a good son," Aunt Hattie said.

Alec shook his head. "I think we'll bypass the pizza joint for something a little more befitting for my favorite aunt. I was thinking the country club or the River House."

Aunt Hattie made a face. "Kind of stuffy. Let's do pizza."

"Are you sure?" Alec asked. Aunt Hattie never failed to surprise him.

"It's a special day," Rory said before he moved on to others in the after-church receiving line. "No matter how you spend it."

"I haven't had pizza in a long time," Aunt Hattie said. "Of course, my doctor will frown on that—but like the preacher said, it is a special day."

"Pizza it is," Alec told her as he helped her into the car. "You know, Mother never even allowed pizza at home. I had to sneak around and grab it when I was out with my friends."

"Your mother surely had her standards," Aunt Hattie replied. "She used to censure what she called my 'wild' impulses. I ignored her for the most part. She loved us, Alec. She just didn't know how to show it."

"I have flowers for her grave," he said. "They're at home. We'll go by and get them after we eat, if that's okay."

"You don't need me to go with you," Aunt Hattie replied, her gaze on church traffic.

"I'd love to have you there if you want," Alec said. "You were as close to her as anyone."

"Then we'll make it special," his aunt said. "We'll take her a slice of pizza."

Alec laughed in spite of the somber moment. "Aunt Hattie, you amaze me."

"I amaze myself at times," his aunt said with a grin. Then she turned serious. "When we get to the pizza place, I want you to tell me all about how you helped the Coast Guard rescue Marla's father and his friends last night. It made the early news this morning."

Alec usually didn't eat at the pizza house during the day, especially on a busy Sunday. The parking lot was almost full with families dressed in everything from church clothes to shorts and flip-flops.

"Looks as if a lot of people had the same idea," Aunt Hattie said. "It is a pretty afternoon now that the rain has stopped."

Alec maneuvered the sedan into a tight parking space and hurried around to help his aunt out of the car. They were headed for the door when he spotted Hunter Lawson's Harley parked by the building.

"Will you look at that?" Aunt Hattie said on a chuckle. "There's a poodle dog on the seat of that big motorcycle."

"That belongs to a friend of mine," Alec admitted.

"The dog or the bike?"

"Both," he said. "The dog is Roxie. We don't know how Hunter wound up with her but she travels everywhere with him."

"He shouldn't leave her all alone out here."

Alec glanced around, looking for Hunter. "You've met him, Aunt Hattie. Hunter Lawson. He doesn't leave her alone. He always sits where he can see her."

They rounded the corner toward the side door. "There he is," Alec said. "Hunter likes to sit out on the deck over the water. He can keep an eye on Roxie from that spot."

"Well, we should say hello."

Alec knew his aunt wouldn't take no for an answer, so he guided her over to where Hunter sat staring out at the water.

"Hi, Lawson."

Hunter turned and gave Alec a quick, hard stare. "Morning." Then he stood up when he saw Aunt Hattie. "Nice to see you again, ma'am."

Aunt Hattie went all girly after hearing that Oklahoma drawl. "Hello, Hunter. You need to come back to our house again soon. We can have another cookout."

Hunter's dark eyes never wavered. "Yes, ma'am."

"I love your dog," Aunt Hattie said, pointing to Roxie.

"She's not my dog." Hunter stood and tossed his paper cup into the trash. "I guess I'd better get going." He brushed past them. "Good to see you again, Miss Hattie." Then he nodded to Alec. "Good job last night."

"Was it something I said?" Aunt Hattie asked after they'd been seated inside by a big window with a water view.

Alec shook his head. "No. We don't know a lot about Hunter. We only know he lost someone he loved and that dog belonged to her."

Aunt Hattie's expression filled with sympathy. "A woman?"

Alec nodded, thinking of last night and little Gabby. "We've all got hidden hurts, don't we?"

"Certainly," his aunt said, some of the luster leaving her eyes. "So tell me about the rescue and…about this developing relationship you have with Marla Hamilton."

Alec stared out at the water much in the same way Hunter had. "I was a hero for fifteen minutes and then I scared little Gabby so badly I had to leave." He leaned close. "And Aunt Hattie, I don't think I can make things work with Marla if I frighten her daughter that way again."

Aunt Hattie shook her head. He'd told her in confidence a little bit about Gabby's fears. "*You* have to get beyond your own fears, Alec. Children are a lot like animals in that way. They can sense when an adult is having anxiety."

"I was kissing her mother," he blurted. "I *was* anxious and excited and…happy. I was happy until I heard that little girl sobbing and screaming for me to get away from her mommy."

"Oh, my," Aunt Hattie said. "That's unfortunate, but you surely aren't going to let that stop you from being a good friend to Marla, are you?"

"I don't have a choice," he said. "That little girl has been through a lot."

"I know," Aunt Hattie said. "You explained, but I've heard the whole story through the church prayer chain."

"You mean gossip?"

"No. I mean deliberate, heartfelt prayers." Aunt Hattie took a sip of her water. "I will keep those prayers going for you, and for Marla and little Gabby. You all deserve to be happy—preferably together."

Alec hadn't realized how much he wanted that until

he heard his aunt stating the obvious. He didn't want to wind up like his buddy Hunter—sitting alone staring out into the water, emotionally unapproachable, except for a little toy poodle named Roxie. And even then, Hunter denied everything.

"I think I might begin looking for a puppy," he said after they started enjoying their fully loaded pizza.

"Will Angus like that?"

"Not for myself," he explained. "But to train for Gabby Hamilton." He was good at helping wounded veterans. Why not try to help a scared little girl, too?

"I hope her mother will agree to that," Aunt Hattie said.

"So do I," Alec replied.

Chapter Sixteen

Brandy met Marla the minute she came downstairs Monday morning. "We have to start preparing for that big fund-raiser. You know, the one with that hunky, mysterious new customer. What's his name?" She poked Marla in the ribs. "Oh, yes. Alec Caldwell."

Marla moaned and put her head in her hands, her elbows slumping on the counter. "That's going to be awkward."

"Why?" Brandy asked, saddling up close, her brown eyes wide with curiosity. "Did you two have a spat?"

Marla wasn't ready to have a girl-to-girl with Brandy. They did share just about everything, but right now, she didn't want to share her feelings regarding Alec with anyone.

"I need more coffee," she said instead. "Gabby didn't want to go to preschool this morning and I'm running late."

"Did she have a bad weekend?" Brandy asked, somehow knowing when to back off on the topic of the hunky, mysterious man.

Marla went straight to the coffee machine and poured

herself a cup. Turning to lean against the long counter lining the wall behind the glass display case, she said, "We all did. My dad went on a fishing charter and the boat got caught in that bad storm."

Brandy immediately stopped piping cookies. "Oh, my. Is everyone okay? I mean, you would have told us if anything bad had happened, but is your dad all right?"

"Other than a sprained arm, he's fine," Marla said on a sigh of relief. "Saturday night was the longest night of my life but he made it home around midnight."

"The roads were flooded everywhere," Brandy said. "I went out with some friends but my mom called and told me to get home. We barely made it."

"That was one of those fast-moving storms," Marla said, her mind on the fast-moving storm brewing in her heart.

She'd thanked God over and over for the Coast Guard and Alec and his friends, but she'd chastised herself for kissing him there in the den at her parents' too-small patio home. She knew better. Gabby didn't always sleep through the night and with all the drama of that night, how could anyone?

Deciding to change the subject, Marla said, "At least Mother's Day turned out nice. We gave Mom her cupcakes, but she was so glad to have my daddy home— that made her day more special than our gifts ever could."

"I can certainly understand that," Brandy said. "I'm so glad everything turned out okay. If you're up to it, let's get to work. Work always makes you feel better. What do you have planned for the Caldwell Canines fund-raiser?"

"I have no idea," Marla admitted, not feeling better

at all. "I think I'll help you get started on today's orders and then I'll go in the office and plan out the dessert menu for the fund-raiser. That's all we have to worry about. Desserts."

Well, she had other things to worry about but that was her problem, not Brandy's. When she thought of how she'd kissed Alec, the word *dessert* took on new meaning. She could probably skip dessert and go right to the kisses.

"Desserts for an estimated three hundred people," Brandy said in her preoccupied, cookie-making fashion.

"Right." Marla didn't know how to handle this. She couldn't cancel on Alec just because he'd kissed her and Gabby had seen them and become upset. She needed the Caldwell account for her business. But she'd never done desserts for that many people—and never under this kind of stress. She didn't need the pressure in her life right now.

She didn't need a man in her life right now.

But Alec wasn't going away.

She needed that Caldwell man…for so many reasons.

She couldn't think about that now. The look of utter hurt and dejection on Alec's face the other night made her wince but the fear in her daughter's cries made her ache. Marla had never been so torn in her life.

Maybe her mother was right. Maybe she'd been protecting Gabby too closely. Being overprotective was just as damaging as not being protective enough. Gabby's therapy had helped her improve, but Marla knew if she wanted her daughter to overcome her anxieties she had to do her part by showing Gabby how to be strong. Since Charlie's death, Marla had sheltered

Gabby to the point of smothering her. No wonder Gabby clung to Marla and her parents like a scared little kitten.

I've been so busy trying to provide a safe life for her, I've neglected actually spending time encouraging her and challenging her to embrace life.

Somehow, she had to find a way to balance things so that Gabby could heal and know that she was loved and would always be protected. And so would Marla. With the clarity of mind that only comes from realizing you've been sleepwalking through life, she suddenly understood that she had to trust in God to give her the same kind of courage she wanted to give her little girl.

Show me how to be strong and brave, Lord.

Her cell rang the minute she walked into the office. Alec.

Did she answer right away? Did she tell him she'd finally figured it all out and that she was willing to go on faith and trust him and God to help her?

What if he was calling to cancel the order? No, Alec wouldn't do that. He was professional about such things and he was a gentleman. He'd honor their agreement and so would she. But she couldn't blurt out the revelation still pounding through her with each heartbeat. Not this way. Not over the phone on a Monday morning when she was still accepting it herself.

Maybe she could ask him to come by later? Or take him some freshly baked cookies. Both of those choices seemed silly and obvious.

"Hello," she said, her voice scratchy.

"Hi. I, uh, I'm so sorry about what happened. I got out of there so I wouldn't scare Gabby any more than I already had."

Marla swallowed her fears, wondering how she could

be upset with herself or Alec. What had happened—that amazing kiss—had happened as naturally as breathing. She'd encouraged Alec, wanted him to stay in spite of her worries for her daughter. Her whole system had buzzed with an awareness she hadn't felt since early in her marriage.

In spite of her fragile daughter sleeping down the hall the other night when they'd kissed.

"It wasn't your fault," she said. "I knew better." She regretted that slip but the words hung in the delicate thread between them like webbed etchings on a wedding cake. Too late to take back those three words. Too late to tell him that she'd had a big change of heart.

He didn't say a word after that comment.

"Alec?"

"Yes, I suppose you did." She heard him clear his throat. "I wanted to make sure you're still willing to help with the fund-raising event. I'd understand if—"

"Of course," she blurted. "I intend to help you, yes. Let's just focus on that, and maybe we can go back to our original plan of being friends."

Another comment that sounded hollow and unsure. She was making a mess of this while her heart knew exactly how to straighten things out.

"Yes, we can try to do that."

The flat tone in his voice didn't sound as if he wanted to try. Marla hated that she'd put that flatness in his mood.

"Unless you feel differently," she said, giving him an out while she held her breath and hoped he wouldn't take it.

"I'm not sure I know what I'm feeling right now," he retorted, the deep huskiness in his voice sliding over her. "I'm glad your dad is okay, and I'm also glad I kissed you. I won't apologize for that, Marla. Ever."

"Alec, I—"

"Just work up a proposal for the cost of your contribution to the event. I appreciate your involvement in the evening."

And then the man ended the call.

Marla could only sit there and stare at the phone. She wondered if they could ever truly be friends. This thing between them wasn't going away. It was only getting stronger in spite of her efforts to hold her feelings, and him, at bay. And now she knew she had to find a way to show Alec that she'd been wrong, so wrong, to fight him at every turn. She longed to call him back and tell him the truth. She'd thought she'd been protecting her daughter, but really, she was the one who was afraid to trust a man again.

Starting tonight after work, she planned to take Gabby out for walks and show her that not everyone in the world was a bad man. And she planned to show Alec that, too.

Somehow.

But right now work had to come first. She'd made him a promise, and she intended to honor that promise no matter how angry or disappointed either of them might feel toward each other. Marla didn't want Alec to be angry with her, but mostly she didn't want to hurt him.

When Marla thought about how Alec had offered to bring a puppy for Gabby to play with, she wondered if she should take him up on that idea. Gabby loved animals but they'd never had a pet of their own. She could just as easily be afraid of a dog, even a puppy, as she was of strangers.

All revelations aside, Marla would have to consider that next step very carefully. She'd talk to Gabby's counselor about it first and she'd continue to encourage, rather than discourage, her daughter. They could finally heal together.

Marla sat down and became lost in creating appropriate cookies and cupcakes for the big event. She'd make bone-shaped and puppy-shaped cookies and ice them with happy doggy faces. She'd create cupcakes with cute names such as Give Me a Treat Caramel or Puppy Love Luscious or maybe Litter of Glitter Gooey. The ideas began to pour out while her heart held on to the discovery of something she'd been missing.

Her faith in God and her faith in Alec.

"Hey, how you doing in here?" Brandy asked from the doorway about an hour later, her big eyes giving Marla a sympathetic stare.

"I'm finally getting some work done," Marla replied. "Did you need something?"

Brandy nodded over her shoulder. "I need your help. We have several customers and Amy's getting behind."

"I'm sorry." Marla jumped up and hurried out to help the part-timer with the line of people waiting at the register. Amy was great with her cashier job, but Marla didn't like to keep any of her customers waiting, so she always pitched in when needed. Brandy was trying to help, too. Which meant she was neglecting the orders that needed to be in the oven. Marla needed to get her head back into the work they had to complete today.

"Good morning, everyone," Marla called to some of her regulars. "Sorry you had to wait."

Her customers were always good-natured about such things and soon they were all laughing and happy. She gave them each a free cookie to show her appreciation. In return, in spite of how she and Alec had ended their conversation, she felt a rush of gratitude that made her ashamed she'd ever had doubts.

God was her strength and her protection even in times of trouble.

Marla only wished she could find a way to tell Alec that.

It was going to be a long day. And a long few weeks before the gala Alec had planned for his philanthropic organization. Marla hoped they'd be able to keep things civil until then. Maybe she could find the right moment to explain to Alec that she wanted him in her life.

Maybe even as more than a friend.

Across town, Alec sat with his board of directors and discussed the plans for the Caldwell Canines Service Dog Association gala to be held in the building he'd purchased. He had a few weeks to clean up the empty shell and at least have the offices and conference room ready. They would work on the dorms, kennels and training areas after the gala. His architect was already working on the floor plans so they could display the whole thing on gala night.

Aunt Hattie attended the board meetings as a member-at-large, probably to give him moral support. She watched him now, a serene expression on her face while her keen eyes took in every nuance of his actions.

She raised a diamond-decked finger. "So we're going to call this the Caldwell Canines Service Dog Association Kennel and Training Facility?"

Alec nodded, his mind still on his brief conversation with Marla. "Yes." He shrugged. "The name is long, I know. But we have to get it all in there."

"You don't sound very enthused," Aunt Hattie replied.

When everyone chuckled in agreement, Alec glanced up and around the room. "Unless someone has a better suggestion."

"It's a little wordy," said one man who'd doubted this whole venture from the start.

"What do you think?" Alec asked Aunt Hattie. She had more good taste in her pinkie than that man had in his entire lineage.

Aunt Hattie leaned forward, one finger curled around her three-strand pearls. "Why not the Alexander and Vivian Caldwell Canine Service Dog Association?"

Surprised, Alec stared over at his aunt. He'd been named after his father and his grandfather, but since his father was rarely talked about when his mother was alive, Alec had never thought of naming the facility after his father. "Would you prefer that name?"

"It's not important what I'd prefer," Aunt Hattie replied. "It's a way of honoring your parents and remembering that your father was a veteran."

Alec swallowed and tried to bite back the heavy dollop of emotions her suggestion brought about. He blinked, cleared his throat and then stared out the window of Caldwell House's formal dining room, where they'd all gathered.

"Alec?"

He looked back at his aunt and saw the love and encouragement in her eyes. "Yes, I think that's a very good idea. Thank you, Aunt Hattie."

"And I'd also suggest we begin to use the acronym to get people familiar with your cause. Goodness, it would take a whole stationery page just to write that title." His aunt patted his arm and then stood, causing every male in the room to do the same. "I'll go start the coffee so we can have refreshments."

The cranky board member who frowned on every subject suddenly sat up straight. "The CCSDA. I like that a lot better. And I approve adding your parents' names in there, too. That's a great honor for them."

Alec glanced down at the agenda and tried to control the roll of something akin to a great wave that moved inside his system. How could he have forgotten that his father had existed and had fought more than a battle with an enemy? His father had been forced to make a great sacrifice for what he believed to be his calling. He'd left his wife and child behind to fight the good fight and he'd sacrificed his life for that fight.

Alec had been chasing his father's broad shadow for most of his life. And he's been hiding behind a facade that wasn't about scars and healing.

He *was* afraid. Afraid of love, afraid of coming out of the shadows and really finding the unconditional love that only the Lord could supply.

He thought of Marla and her little girl, his heart hurting when he remembered how frightened Gabby had been to see him with her mother.

Alec held that same fright but he was willing to fight for a woman like Marla. In order to do that, he'd have to step out and find that light that would shine deep into his soul, where the real scars still festered.

He wanted to tell Marla that he understood now.

He truly understood.

But she'd probably never want to deal with him again.

Unless he could find a way to prove to her that he needed to heal completely before he could love completely.

Chapter Seventeen

—

Marla went back over what the therapist had taught her about introducing Gabby to new situations. It had worked when the therapist had guided them through some role-playing. She prayed it would work now. "Remember, honey, we might see some big people today. People besides Pawpaw and Memaw and your teachers at preschool and church school."

"Who?" Gabby played with her new stuffed dog. Another suggestion from her therapist to help her feel safe.

"Remember Mr. Dipsey? He looks a lot like Santa, right?"

Gabby nodded and stuck her lip out in a frowning pout. "He rides a cart like Pawpaw but he tried to tickle me."

"Yes, and he wants to wave to you—not tickle you—so you and Pawpaw and Memaw are going for a ride around the neighborhood. You'll be safe with Pawpaw. I want you to wave to Mr. Dipsey. He's a Pawpaw, too. He has three grandchildren."

"Do they like him?"

Marla stared down at Gabby's big, trusting brown

eyes. "They love him in the same way you love Paw-paw." She touched a hand to Gabby's hair. "Do you think you could smile and wave to Mr. Dipsey without getting upset or scared? He's a really nice man."

"I'll try."

That was better than running to her bed and hiding her face. Marla breathed a sigh of relief and prayed this would work. Mom had already been practicing, now with Marla's permission, but after that episode with Alec, Marla knew if she ever wanted to move on she had to help her daughter do the same.

Gabby deserved to know love and happiness when she got older. Marla intended to show her both so they could perhaps move on to the puppy therapy Alec had suggested.

"The puppy therapy works in most cases," Gabby's counselor had told Marla at their last appointment. "If you want her to meet this new man in your life, you need him and the puppy in the same room. When Gabby sees the puppy, she'll trust the animal first. But she'll warm up to your friend, too, if things go the way they should."

"And what if they don't?"

"We keep trying," the therapist replied. "Just have your friend stand back and stay quiet for a while. Then you can engage him in conversation about the animal. Gabby will decide if she can trust him or not and when that time comes, you'll know by the way she reacts whether it's working or not."

Marla wanted to keep trying—and not just because she wanted to spend more time with Alec. Meeting him had certainly been the catalyst that had woken her up to her own needs, but she'd tried several different

forms of therapy with her daughter to help Gabby overcome her anxieties. Some had worked, and some needed
more time and patience—she was afraid the dog therapy might be one of those. But time and patience could
work in her favor, too. She had to be sure about Alec,
about taking on a puppy and about protecting and encouraging her daughter.

Mom came into the bedroom where Gabby and
Marla sat. "Ready for our special ride?"

Gabby hopped up and grabbed her little stuffed dog.
"Barky is going with us."

"Barky." Mom shrugged at Marla. "I love that name."

"He really barks." Gabby pushed at Barky's belly
and the little dog made a *woof, woof* sound.

"And so he does," Mom said, her smile full of reas-
surance. "You can make him bark at Mr. Dipsey. He
might fall out of his golf cart."

Gabby giggled and hugged Barky close. "I wish
Barky was real."

Mom gave Marla a hopeful glance.

"How would you like a real puppy?" Marla ventured,
her heart bumping into a jitter.

"I'd love it!" Gabby jumped up and down, threw her
stuffed puppy in the air and then caught him again.

Marla leaned down to her level. "I know a very nice
man who might be able to let you play with a special
puppy."

Gabby's eyes widened, fright evident in her expression. "A scary man?"

"No," Marla replied. "You saw him here the other
night. He was hugging me, remember?"

Gabby shook her head. "I don't like that man."

Mom tried. "Gabby, that man was hugging Mommy

because we'd all been so worried about Pawpaw. He helped get Pawpaw out of that bad storm. He's a very kind man who would never do anything to hurt Mommy or you. He takes care of other people and helps them find good doggies to protect them and love them. And he knows all about puppies and how to help little girls."

Gabby held Barky tight and shook her head. "I don't know if I want to see that man again."

"It's all right, honey," Marla said. "You don't have to do anything that you don't like." Then she remembered what she had to do. "But Mr. Dipsey is safe and friendly. So you need to learn to speak to him and at least greet him with a smile."

Mom took Gabby by the hand. "Let's go. We don't want to miss letting Barky woof at Mr. Dipsey. He'll ride by and wave but we aren't going to talk to him at all." Then she leaned down. "I'll tell you more about Alec. He's the nice man who might be able to find you a cute *real* puppy. But we have to try not to be upset with him."

Marla watched as they hurried out and held her hands across her stomach. She'd tried so hard to be patient. They'd nurtured Gabby through the past year with lots of hugs and reassurances, but while her parents had encouraged Gabby to heal, Marla knew she'd held back, afraid of pushing Gabby too fast.

What if Gabby never healed? What if her daughter had anxieties the rest of her life because of one incident that she could never fully understand?

I have to trust in the Lord, she reminded herself.

She'd decided that and she'd stick to it. But Marla also knew that the Lord needed her to do her part. And that meant gently pushing Gabby to be brave and to find the good in people.

Including Alec Caldwell.

Alec went back over the floor plans for what would become the Alexander and Vivian Caldwell Canines Service Dog Association. The architect had done a good job of accessing the building and the acreage behind it.

"Paul, could we add a few more dorm rooms?" Alec asked, turning to his friend. "I want as many veterans and others in need as possible to be able to stay here while they train with their animals. We'll need easy accessibility for those with disabilities, too, of course."

Paul Whitman was in his late forties and married with four daughters. He laughed and nodded. "I know all about dorm rooms, Alec. Two in high school and two in grad school."

Alec patted Paul on the back. "I admire you. And that's why I hired you."

Paul made some notes on his electronic pad. "Girls are hard to learn, Alec. A lot of drama there."

"I can only imagine." Alec pushed away thoughts of Marla and how undramatic she was. He had work to do, and he intended to keep busy day and night so he wouldn't think about the woman who'd come into his life in such a soft, stealthy way.

Holding the remains of a wedding cake.

But not wanting to ever walk down the aisle with anyone again.

He'd been abrupt with her the last time they'd talked and now he regretted that with the same intensity Paul would probably regret going shoe shopping with his daughters. Alec didn't know how to fix things between

Marla and him. Maybe things couldn't be fixed or didn't need to be fixed. He'd see her at the gala in a couple of weeks, so he'd steel himself against not seeing her a minute before.

But when he heard a female laugh echoing throughout the empty open building, his heart did a little bump that only reinforced how much he missed Marla. He whirled from the foldout table where the blueprints were spread and glanced toward the glass doors at the front of the long building.

High heels clipped against the concrete.

"Alec, darling, there you are."

So not Marla.

"Hey, Annabelle," Paul said before giving Alec a quick questioning glance. "How ya doing, kiddo?"

"I'm fine," Annabelle said through the fog of a sweetly scented floral perfume. She gave Paul a chaste hug and then opened her arms wide toward Alec. "So good to see you again. I see our little project is coming to fruition. I'm so excited about being a part of this."

Alec tried to form both a smile and a thought, but Annabelle just kept right on talking. "When I saw your cars here, I just had to stop by and see how things are progressing. The buzz is that this gala will be *the* event of the summer. I can't wait to see the invitations."

Alec didn't miss the hint of suggestion in that assumption. He'd have to invite the woman since she'd helped him broker the sale, but he dreaded that shrill, exaggerated drawl moving through the crowd all night. He tried not to compare this stunning woman to Marla. But there was no comparison in his mind. Marla was pretty, sweet and unassuming.

And in spite of what he had thought or believed about

himself before, he liked those qualities. Because meeting Marla had shown him a different kind of woman.

"Alec?"

He came out of his dreams and saw Annabelle staring at him with a fixed smile on her red lips. "I do hope I get to dance with you at the gala."

"The dance floor will be open," he said. "I have someone working on finding a good jazz ensemble."

"Jazz?" She made a face. "I like fast music."

Paul gave Alec what might have been a sympathetic glance but refrained from joining the conversation.

Alec chuckled and tugged at his ear. "I'll make sure we include a few upbeat numbers." Then he gently took Annabelle by her skinny elbow. "Was there any other reason you stopped by?"

If his question stung, she recovered quickly. "Do I have to have a reason? I wondered if you'd be at the Rotary Club lunch." Her blue-eyed gaze fluttered like a butterfly over Paul and Alec. "You know how I hate being one of the few females there."

"I hope to be there, yes. Paul and I both plan on attending."

"Good. Then I can sit between y'all."

Paul started rolling up blueprints. "I'll get right on these changes, Alec. Got to get back to the office and handle some other pressing matters. Annabelle, always good to see you."

Coward. Alec shook Paul's hand and thanked him. After his friend left, he turned back to Annabelle. "It was nice to see you today. I have a lunch meeting, so let me escort you out."

"I was hoping *we* could have lunch," Annabelle said,

her blond curls reminding him of fingers curling toward him.

"I'm sorry. I can't make it today. This project has me running twenty-four-seven."

"So I hear," she said on a tight little note. "Running by the pastry shop or out to the retirement village. Who in the world do you know at those boring old places, anyway?"

Enough was enough.

"And who in the world would bother gossiping to you about both of those places?"

She looked shocked. "I hear things. See things. Think things."

"Then maybe you should become more like the three little monkeys. Hear no evil, see no evil, speak no evil."

"What are you implying, Alec Caldwell?"

"I'm not implying anything except this, Annabelle— I don't listen to gossip and I don't like gossip. It's especially annoying and unbecoming from such a lovely person. You're above that kind of behavior, surely?"

Annabelle wasn't sure how to answer that so she just giggled. "Of course. It's just that, well, you know— that Hamilton woman isn't used to moving in Caldwell circles."

Alec's pulse paced in much the same way it had whenever he'd been in the middle of combat. His aunt had a saying that there were all kinds of enemies in this world and some of them smiled when they went in for the kill. Annabelle was certainly doing that right now.

"Marla Hamilton is a good friend of mine and she's also helping with some of the food for the gala. You should consider using her services at the next Realtors meeting at the chamber of commerce. The best cookies and cupcakes in the world."

"I'll try to remember that." Annabelle tugged at her heavy purse and fluffed her hair. "Got to go. If you won't have lunch with me, I guess it will be another salad at my desk. I've sworn off sweets."

Ouch. The claws were out.

Alec watched as she strolled out the door with her pride still very much intact. He was proud of himself for not escorting her out and locking the door behind her. At least this time, Marla hadn't seen Annabelle hugging him close.

Not that it mattered, really. After the gala he'd probably never see Marla that much again. She'd be done with him. But that didn't mean he could go back to a woman like Annabelle, either.

"I'm spoiled," Alec mumbled to himself as he moved through the location that would become a big part of his future. He longed to call Marla and tell her about all his plans. He wanted to stop by the bakery and get some cookies for dessert or maybe order a sandwich made with freshly baked bread.

He *was* spoiled. He would never swear off sweets again.

But Alec knew Marla needed time. He knew this from his own experience with a traumatic event. It had taken him a long time to reach out to others, to get up and clean up and put on a suit and tie and begin the work his mother had left for him to do.

Did you know, Mother? Did you know I'd need something to make me whole again?

His mother might have left Alec a legacy, but Vivian Caldwell had no idea that he'd found something—

someone—much more important than any legacy he could cultivate.

He'd found a woman who understood what it was like to do something good with your life. A woman with whom he could build something solid and strong. Marla.

If only he could help her find her own path to healing.

Chapter Eighteen

Why was it when she was trying so hard to avoid a man, he showed up everywhere?

Marla had seen Alec in church and at the Farmer's Market. She'd run into him on downtown streets and at various restaurants. And each time she saw him, her heart hurt with the sure knowledge that she was falling for him. But each time, they'd engaged in small talk and awkward moments that only left her confused and dazed. How could she continue to function like this—dejected and defeated, and wishing for something she couldn't have?

Today, Alec and his three buddies were taking over the badly wilted and half-dead community garden out at the Millbrook Lake Retirement Village. Her father had called her out here, too, with the excuse that the summer sun was killing off what was left of his prized tomato plants.

Or so he'd said.

"What are you doing?" she asked Alec, her gardening gloves held tight to her chest. He looked too good to be digging in a garden. His dark T-shirt showed off his biceps and his smile only reinforced the attraction that zoomed through her like a hummingbird fluttering its wings.

"What do you mean, what am I doing?" His smile held a touch of longing. His amber eyes warmed her hotter than the golden rays of sunshine streaming across the trees.

"I mean, you're here, in this garden."

Alec laughed and hit the hoe he'd been carrying against the soft dirt of a long row of ripe tomatoes. "I promised your dad we'd help out with this garden. Rory called me and asked if we'd like to come out today. Apparently, he needs people with the ability to weed out the bad stuff."

"Unbelievable," Marla said. She shoved on her gloves and decided to get her work done and get out of here. "I'm a picker. I get to pick all of these ripening tomatoes."

"We all have to sacrifice," he quipped with a wink. Then his expression changed to something soft and yielding and open. "How have you been?"

Marla thought about the question while she glared at her smug daddy. Should she tell Alec that sometimes she couldn't sleep because she was remembering being in his arms? Or that she'd thought about what it would be like to have an open, easy relationship with him? One where her daughter would giggle and look up at Alec with adoring eyes?

"I've been okay," she said. "How about you?"

"Good. Busy." He glanced to where three other men were getting out of an old Jeep and taking directions from Dipsey. One of them was Preacher Rory Sanderson. "The facility renovations are coming along.

We've got the main lobby area and the offices ready for the gala. I've hired a decorator to make it *festive*." He grinned and swiped a hand over his clipped hair. "And the dorms are being built, too. The training yard will come next. I can't wait to show it to you."

Marla loved the passion she saw in his eyes and she loved that he wanted to show her what he cared about the most. "I'm happy for you. You've certainly worked hard to make this a reality."

"Yes." He hit the hoe against a few parched weeds and what was left of a bean stalk. "I wanted to ask you something—"

"Hey, man, don't hold up the row."

Alec glanced past Marla, impatience in his voice. "Blain, get your own row. I've already claimed this one."

The man whom Alec had spoken to ignored the suggestion and came closer. "Hey," he said to Marla. "I'm Blain Kent. I came with him, but don't let that scare you."

Shocked at his words, Marla glanced from him back to Alec. But the smirk on Alec's face alleviated her concerns. Man-talk was so different from woman-speak. "Okay," she said, smiling. "I've heard a lot about you, Blain."

"All good, I'm sure." Blain's dark blue eyes looked like midnight diamonds. A real heartbreaker of a guy. And a really dedicated detective, from what Alec had told her.

"All good," she assured him. "It's nice to meet you."

"And you know me, of course." Rory Sanderson gave Marla a quick hug. "I saw your dad yesterday and he invited me to come and dig in the dirt. I brought a few friends."

"So I can blame you for this," Marla said, giving him a mock frown. How could she be mad at a man she admired and appreciated for helping her in her faith struggle?

"Blame away," Preacher said. "I can handle it."

She believed that. "Well, I appreciate all of you coming out here on a Sunday afternoon to help clear up what's left of this garden."

"And a warm afternoon," Blain said, wiping at his dark bangs. He motioned to the friend who'd been driving the Jeep. "Looks like Lawson's gonna finish his row before we ever get started."

Marla watched as the mysterious Lawson, whom Alec had mentioned, hit his hoe to dirt and slung weeds and old plants as if there was a fire behind him. "He's very efficient," she said.

"And Roxie's doing her part," Rory pointed out. "She's digging in the dirt."

Marla laughed at the cute little poodle following the dark-haired, unsmiling man, who was hurrying up a row of dead lima-bean stalks. "That is the cutest dog I've ever seen."

"Roxie," Blain said on a whisper. "She's little, but fierce."

They talked a little bit more, but soon everyone settled into work. Marla picked what tomatoes she could save and left the rest for Alec to hoe away. The Florida heat and humidity made having a summer garden a hard task, but her daddy knew all of the planting seasons and planted accordingly. Soon, he'd have a fall garden going in this same spot.

"Where's Gabby today?" Alec asked, coming up behind her.

"With my mom at the community pool," Marla said. "She's learning to swim. I took her for a couple of hours yesterday. She loves the beach, too, but we don't get out there as much."

"How's she doing?"

Marla stopped and dropped a plump tomato into the bucket she'd been carrying up the row. "She's getting better." She took off her gloves for a minute. "We're slowly introducing her to more people." At the look of regret in his eyes, she added, "And Alec, we've talked to her about you and shown her pictures of you."

Like the photo Marla had seen recently in the *Millbrook Messenger*. The local paper had highlighted the Caldwell Foundation and the opening of the service dog training facility. The gala was the talk of the town, which the article highlighted, and there had been a photo of Alec in front of the facility, a smile on his face. A beautiful smile that hid his scar and showcased his enthusiasm for this project.

That smile dimmed now. "How does she react when you mention me?"

"She's getting used to the idea of you being one of the good guys."

He lowered his head, his gaze holding hers. "I want to be one of the good guys," he said as his breath caught. "I miss you, Marla."

Marla's heart slipped and slid back into place. "I miss you, too. I think we lost something when we moved too fast."

"Yeah, we lost us. Our friendship, our talks, our

meals together. Just being with each other. I miss your smile, and I really miss your cupcakes."

She slapped at his arm with one of her gloves. "You have an open invitation for free cupcakes. Just come by and see me anytime."

"I might do that." He started tugging at vines and weeds. "I know you've got everything in order regarding the desserts for the gala, but—"

"I'll deliver them a couple of hours before the event," she said, her stomach roiling with apprehension. What if she messed up on this? "I want everything to be fresh."

"I know, and I appreciate that, but—"

"Hey, break time!"

Alec let out a groan and turned to see Dipsey waving to them. "I don't need a break."

Marla wondered why he seemed so irritated. "Are you upset that we've been talking you up to Gabby?"

He leaned on his hoe and stared into her eyes. "No. I'm aggravated because I've been trying to ask you if you'd be my date for the gala and I get interrupted at every turn."

Marla's pulse stopped and then sputtered back into a fast rhythm. "You want me to what?"

"I want y'all to come and get some lemonade," her dad said from right behind her.

Marla turned so fast, she almost tripped over her tomato bucket. Alec caught her and drew her close. The scent of something spicy and rich merged with good, honest sweat. Marla resisted the urge to reach up and touch his forehead.

He gave her a direct stare that held a hint of a plea. "Can we go somewhere later and talk—just talk?"

"Absolutely," she said, her face inches from his. "And I'll make sure I wash the tomato smell off before we do."

"I love tomatoes," he said before he released her.

"I think you two need some lemonade," her dad said with a smile.

"Mom, I won't be too late getting back."

"Take your time," Mom said with her usual calm. "Your dad is off with his friends, watching a baseball game. So I will enjoy the company of Miss Gabby here."

"I get to spend all day with Memaw," Gabby pointed out. "Even the dark parts."

"Yes, even the dark parts," Mom said on a giggle. "We'll read books and watch princess movies and eat too much popcorn."

"Thank you," Marla said. "I don't know what I'd do without you."

"That's why we're here," Mom said. "Stop worrying."

Marla left to go back to her apartment to get cleaned up. It wasn't every weekend she asked her mom to keep Gabby extra time, so why did she feel so guilty?

Because each time she left her little girl, she remembered the one day she'd been unable to pick up Gabby. The day her husband had died and her daughter had been traumatized.

How will I ever get over that day, Lord?

Thoughts of Alec came into her head. He wanted her to go to the gala as his date. *The gala*. Just thinking about all those fancy, glamorous patrons mixing and mingling scared her silly.

Not to mention being with Alec that night. How could she say yes? How could she say no?

When she'd mentioned it to her mother, Joyce had clapped her hands with glee. "Go, honey. It's not often a girl gets to be Cinderella."

"But what will I do when the clock strikes midnight, Mom?"

"Hold on to your shoes," Mom retorted with a grin.

Then her mother had insisted that yes, she should meet Alec tonight to discuss this further. Joyce Reynolds, ever the romantic matchmaker.

But Marla did want to see Alec tonight. And that was probably where her guilt hit her the hardest. Guilt over her husband's death. Guilt over their troubled marriage. Guilt over her daughter's fragility. And guilt over being attracted to a man who scared her in ways she'd never imagined.

But, amazingly, Gabby hadn't cringed or pouted at the mention of his name.

Marla had approached the subject with her daughter. "So, Mommy's going to go out to dinner with Mr. Alec tonight. You know him now, right?"

"The man in the newspaper?"

"Yes, that man."

"He likes dogs," Gabby said, Barky close to her on the couch. "I like dogs, too."

"He sure does. He's going to help place some special dogs with some people who need help."

"That's nice."

"Yes, he's a good man. He even told me he could find a puppy for us. For you to have as your very own."

"Memaw likes him a lot." Gabby held Barky close again. "I like puppies, Mommy. Will he bring me one?"

"Yes, he can bring you one. But I don't want you to

be upset or afraid of Mr. Alec. Maybe one day you can meet him again."

"Maybe. And I can meet my puppy, too."

Now Marla thanked God for that one small bit of progress.

She hurried into the shower and got dressed in jeans and a short-sleeved T-shirt. Casual. This was a casual date.

After drying her hair, she left it down and touched some pink gloss to her lips.

When she heard the knock at the door, she took a calming breath. This might be their first official date so she wanted to enjoy it.

What would it be like if she went with him to the gala?

What would that mean, being seen with him in front of the whole town? It could open up a whole new world, or it could turn out to be a world of hurt.

Marla opened the door and took in the sight of him. He wore a T-shirt and jeans, too. And a sweet smile.

"Hi."

"Hi." She waved him inside.

"You look nice." His gaze moved from her to the small living room and kitchen. "I like this apartment."

Marla glanced around at the mismatched, second-hand furniture her mom had helped her refurbish. Her place was sparse but colorful and she had a nice view of the canal that merged with the river and the lake. "Thanks. It works for now."

He stood with his hands in the pocket of his jeans. "Are you ready to go?"

"Sure." She grabbed her purse.

Alec opened the door for her but stopped and shut it again. "Marla?"

"What?" Had he changed his mind?

"Just this."

He pulled her into his arms and kissed her, his hands pulling through her hair.

He lifted his head and feathered tiny kisses down her cheekbone. "I…I needed to do that. I needed to kiss you."

"Okay." She swallowed and tried to find her balance again. This felt perfect, being in his arms. "All right."

"All right, good? Or all right, bad?"

"Good," she managed to say on a husky whisper.

He kissed her again. "Good," he repeated. Then with a peck on her forehead, he took her hand and hauled her out the door. "We've moved beyond friendship, Marla."

"I can live with that," she said.

She wanted to live with that. If only Gabby would be able to do the same.

Chapter Nineteen

Marla's heartbeat had accelerated a couple of beats with each shift of the gears of the sports car. They were headed away from town, out toward the big bay. Alec had the top down but he took his time, allowing the wind to play across Marla's skin and lift her hair out behind her. Since she was still reeling from that kiss, the warm wind cooled her and helped clear her head.

"Where are we going?" she asked, anticipation moving through her as they zoomed along the road that followed the river.

He maneuvered a curve with ease and glanced over at her. "It's a surprise."

"Oh. Okay."

"Do you like surprises?"

"Sometimes." She thought of the horror of finding her husband shot and her child with a frightened salesclerk. "I like the good kind."

"This is the good kind." He reached for her hand and squeezed it.

His touch shot through Marla with a reassuring strength. "I thought maybe you were kidnapping me.

That maybe you're really a pirate with a big ship waiting out beyond the shoreline."

"You have a vivid imagination."

Yes, but he hadn't argued about the pirate part. And she wasn't exactly refusing to go with him.

"It's a nice night," she said, hoping to draw him out more.

"Yes. A perfect night for a picnic."

"A picnic?" She glanced around. "This car is too small to hold a picnic basket."

He grinned at that comment. "It has a nice trunk."

"Oh." She hadn't thought of that. What did she know about fancy convertibles?

"Where are we going for this picnic?"

"To a special place."

"And do you take everyone to this place?"

"No. I've never brought a woman there."

"Is this your camp, Alec?"

"It's not just my camp, but yes. Well—we won't go to the house, but we'll be near the camp house."

"So I'm not allowed to venture into your man cave?"

"No girls allowed. But, trust me, you don't want to go in there. It's not fit for feminine eyes."

She laughed into the wind. "Okay, then. A picnic near your camp house. I'm intrigued."

"I think you'll like it."

When he pulled up to the square house built high on thick round pilings, she could see Millbrook Bay shimmering out in the distance.

"I haven't been out to this bay in a while," she said. "With work and trying to spend time with Gabby, I don't get to see much of the big water around Millbrook."

"Well, tonight you'll get to do just that." He pointed up. "Look at that moon."

The full moon hung like a giant pearl up in the sky. It cast a luminous creamy glow across the dark water.

"It's beautiful," she said. She opened her door to get out but Alec was right there to help her, his hand holding hers in a warm embrace.

Marla chatted to hide her jumbled nerves. "So what did you bring for us to eat on this moonlight picnic?"

He laughed at that and hit a button on the key fob to open the trunk. "Honestly, Aunt Hattie insisted on preparing and packing the food. She was appalled that I'd planned peanut butter and jelly sandwiches and boxed cookies."

"Sounds exactly like what I'm used to," Marla said, thinking how adorable he would look making a sandwich.

Adorable and too close to the perfect image of a loving husband and father. A shard of longing shot through her, its glistening heat matching the moon's glow over the water.

He lifted a small straw basket and what looked like a blanket. "Well, I guess my genteel aunt thought better of that notion. Aunt Hattie wouldn't want us to have an ordinary, everyday picnic."

Marla took his free hand and together they walked past the house and down to a dock out over the water. The bay's gentle waves lapped at the shore with a soft cadence. The night wind lifted over them, balmy and quiet. Somewhere along the shoreline, a bird called out.

"Now what?" she asked, afraid she'd wake up from a nice dream.

He set down the basket. "Well, here's our picnic blanket. So we won't get splinters." He spread the colorful quilt across the weathered planks. "I think my aunt even packed bug spray, in case the mosquitoes want to join us."

"Your Aunt Hattie is such a thoughtful person," Marla said. "She's kind to everyone she meets."

"We could all take a lesson from that."

Marla helped him spread the quilt. Then he took her hand and they sat down with their backs against a built-in bench.

She noticed when he winced. "We can sit on the bench if it bothers your leg, Alec."

"It's okay. I'm sore from all that work your dad put me through." He grinned over at her. "It's more my back than my leg."

"Thank you for helping," she said. "The garden looks great now. He'll till it and get it ready for the fall planting."

"I think I got volunteered to help with that, too."

He opened the basket and started pulling out carefully wrapped food. "Oh, I love you, Aunt Hattie."

Hearing Alec says those words stirred Marla's heart with a bittersweet twist. "What did she send with you?"

"Her honey-baked ham. I mean, she knows me so well. She cooks it every few months or so and she knows I love a good ham sandwich with this particular ham. And she put Swiss cheese on here, too. With tomatoes from your dad's garden."

"A feast." Marla lost her heart over a ham sandwich.

"And fresh strawberry lemonade."

"I'm a blessed woman."

He laughed and brought out two cups so he could pour from the big flower-embossed thermos. "I think she also packed two slices of zucchini bread. She believes in something healthy at every meal."

"So do I," Marla said between bites of her sandwich. "Since I live with sweets all the time, I have to be careful."

"You look great to me, but I want you healthy, too."

He'd said that in such a way that it suggested a permanent relationship. Marla finished her sandwich and sat back to break off chunks of the moist bread. "Thank you," she said, her voice quiet with emotion.

Alec sat back, too, and stretched his wounded leg out in front of him. "You never answered me this afternoon. So let me do this again." He turned to her and smiled. "Will you attend the gala with me?"

Every instinct told Marla to say no. But her heart shouted to her that if she turned him down, she might lose Alec forever.

She'd been ready to take the next step. To move into a relationship with him. But the thought of stepping out into such a broad spotlight, with just about everyone in town seeing them together, caused her to panic. She wasn't sure she was ready for that kind of exposure. Why couldn't she do as she'd decided and turn this over to God?

"Marla?" He shifted to face her, one hand touching on her cheekbone. "I want you to be there—out front, and not just behind-the-scenes."

"Some people are meant to stay behind-the-scenes."

"Is that why you're being so hesitant? Are you afraid of crowds? Or just afraid of being with me?"

"I'm afraid I'll disappoint you," she said. There, that was out in the open. The source of all her doubts and fears.

His hand stilled on her cheek. "How could you ever disappoint me?"

"Alec, look at me. I'm not like…that beautiful blonde I saw you with when you first looked at the place. I'm just plain ol' Marla Hamilton."

"You're more than that," he said. "Marla, you run your own business and take care of a very special little girl. You work hard and you're one of those kind people, like my Aunt Hattie. I could see that the first time I met you." He shook his head. "Don't compare yourself to Annabelle or anyone else."

Hot tears pricked at her eyes. "But what if I don't fit in? I tried to fit into my husband's world and I felt as if I always fell short. I don't want to lose you because we have such different lifestyles."

"This isn't about a lifestyle," Alec said, a trace of frustration coloring his words. "This is about us, you and me, here right now, and how we feel about each other. Forget the rest of it."

"But there is more," she said, her heart hurting while she poured out her worst fears. "What if…I fall for you, but Gabby can't accept you in my life? I saw how hurt you were that night she woke up and saw you. I won't put you through that, Alec. It's not fair."

"None of this is fair," he retorted. "But we have to trust in God. We have to start somewhere."

Marla knew he was right. "I've wanted to tell you so many times that I've finally seen that. That I have to ask for God's help and grace in this. He can fix what I can't fix but…"

"But you're still afraid to let go and see this through?"

She bobbed her head. "I thought I was ready. And I

am ready to trust you and to work toward bringing you and Gabby together."

"But not yet," he said, one arm thrown over his bent knee. "Not enough to go public with me and stand by me when I need someone there the most."

Heartbroken, Marla realized that Alec needed her with him. That he'd found a way to get past his own scars to trust her. Why couldn't she make this final step toward what she wanted with all of her heart? Toward the one person that God had brought into her life for a purpose?

When she didn't respond, Alec stood and lifted her up. He sat on the bench with her, pain coloring his eyes. "I guess that's a no, then."

"Alec, I—"

"It's okay," he said, reaching down to put away the remains of their meal. "I understand—really, I do."

But she could tell he didn't understand and Marla knew by the way he became quiet and distant, that it was too late to tell him she'd go with him. Because he needed her there.

"Alec?"

"Don't say anything." He rolled up the quilt and tucked it under his arm. "I know all the reasons, but that doesn't mean I have to accept them."

With that, he guided her back to the car, put away the picnic basket and silently got in on the driver's side.

Marla wanted to scream into the night. Why did this have to be so difficult? Why was she letting the best man she'd ever known slip out of her life?

Because she knew she'd either lose him now when they were still struggling or she'd lose him later. When it would hurt much worse. How could she blame Alec for walking away? She'd hurt him with her excuses and her own fears. Would she wind up hurting him over and over if they took things to the next level?

Marla wanted to stop making excuses but she couldn't take the next step with Alec. Not yet. Not until her heart caught up with her head and she knew she could finally love again. Just like her little girl, she was holding back out of fear and dread.

How could she ever make him see that she wanted to be there by his side? Not just for a night, but for a lifetime and beyond.

Chapter Twenty

Alec went through the motions of getting ready for the fund-raising event, but his heart wasn't really co-operating with all the business decisions his head kept telling him he needed to take care of.

"Where do you want these tables?"

Alec turned to find a delivery man from the events company standing there with a clipboard.

"Tables." Alec looked out over the vast empty space that would soon be active with people. "Line them up over near the big windows."

The man nodded and scribbled on his pad. "And the serving tables? For the food?"

Thoughts of Marla invaded Alec's mind, filling him with such a bittersweet pain that he had to clear his throat. "Why don't you place them underneath the area by the reception desk." He pointed to the bright red counter the workmen had finished a few days ago. "Leave room for the servers to stand behind the tables, please."

"Yes, sir."

The man went off to take care of his business while Alec stood here dreading the rest of the day.

"You won't get much done standing there staring out the window."

He turned to find Rory Sanderson coming across the room. "Hi."

"Wow, what an enthusiastic hello."

Alec shot his friend a weak smile. "Sorry. Got a lot on my mind."

Rory nodded, his hands on his hips. "Yep, I reckon you do. Missed you at church last Sunday."

"Sorry. I was…tired."

"And you didn't make it to the Wednesday lunch, either."

Alec rubbed a hand down his face. "What day is it, anyway?"

"Okay, that's it. You and me are out of here."

"I don't have time—"

"Nonsense. Take off that tie and come with me. Preacher's orders."

"We're not on base anymore, Rory."

"No. We're on God's time and God wants you to take a break."

Alec decided he'd waste more time arguing with Preacher than just giving in and getting this pep talk over with. "All right, already. Let me call my assistant."

"I'll be outside," Rory said.

Alec let everyone know he was leaving for lunch, then loosened his tie and rolled up his shirt sleeves. When he got outside, he saw Blain's Jeep. With Blain, Preacher and even Hunter waiting. Roxie was sitting with Rory and him on the backseat.

"What's going on?" he asked, frowning.

"An intervention," Blain said from the driver's seat.

Alec reluctantly hopped in next to Blain. "I can't spend all day letting all of you *intervene* on me. I don't need this and I have a lot to do before the gala this weekend."

"It'll get done, man," Blain said. "Look at that sky. As blue as my ex-girlfriend's eyes."

"And way more calm," Rory offered.

Lawson grunted and scratched Roxie's fluffy little white-haired head.

"Where are we going?" Alec asked, remembering Marla had asked him that same thing last weekend. He hadn't talked to her since their ill-fated picnic. His new assistant was taking care of all the details of the gala.

"Burgers," Rory said. "We need us some big, juicy burgers."

"It's always about food." Alec hit his hand against the dashboard. "We meet and eat, and that's supposed to make everything great. Well, it doesn't." Not even a cupcake could fix his bad mood.

"Bayside Burgers," Blain said with a grin.

Bayside Burgers. An old shack of a restaurant out past the lake on the big water. The place had survived storms and floods and too many spring break partiers. Alec didn't miss the implied message. Survival. They'd all survived war and death and chaos.

Surely he could survive this?

Alec finally smiled and gave in. "Well, now, that's a different matter." He'd listen to his friends but he wasn't sure what more he could do to win over Marla.

Blain shifted gears as they headed out of town.

Marla glared at the burned loaf of strawberry bread that sat smoking on the big stainless-steel counter.

"How could I let this happen?" she mumbled to herself. "Mrs. Philpott needed this for her circle meeting tonight."

"You're distracted," Brandy said.

"I'm busy," Marla replied, wondering how Brandy always heard everything, even things she hadn't really voiced.

"You should have said yes to the dress."

"Excuse me?"

"You should have said yes to Dreamy McMarine." Brandy lifted the bread and put it out of sight. "You know, new dress, new shoes, new man in your life. Every woman's dream, all in one night."

"We've had this discussion," Marla replied, her body and soul so zapped she wanted to sit in a corner and cry. But she didn't have that luxury. She had to finish the cookies and cakes and everything else she'd promised to deliver to the Caldwell Canines facility on Saturday afternoon. Two days away and she was still scrambling to get things done.

"We've had this discussion, yes," Brandy said. "And you know we'll get everything done. We have all of the cupcakes baked and we'll ice them Saturday morning. The little Bundt cakes are done and ready to serve. The adorable doggy cookies are baking right now and we'll ice them later today when our part-timers get here. So all you need to worry about is your dress, your shoes and letting me do your hair and makeup."

"I'm not going," Marla retorted, agitation making her snap. "I have to make more strawberry bread."

Brandy let out a long-suffering sigh. "I don't get it."

"It's not yours to get," Marla said. "I have my reasons."

"I still don't get it."

Brandy pranced off before Marla could tell her to leave her alone. Her young assistant meant well—as did her mother and her father and just about anyone else who'd asked her if she would be attending the big event.

No, she wouldn't. She couldn't. She'd decided she'd have to give up on having a future with Alec Caldwell. Some things weren't meant to be. Her own doubts and fears were holding her back. But her heart screamed at her to go for it. To take a chance. She'd fallen in love with Alec, but that didn't necessarily mean she could have a life with him. And her prayers seemed superficial compared to what Alec had been through and what the people he wanted to help had suffered.

I just need to get over myself and get on with my work.

When the bell chime on the shop's front door jingled, Marla glanced up. Hattie Marshall walked in, a double strand of pearls glistening around her neck.

"Hello, Marla," Aunt Hattie said from across the counter. "How are you today?"

"I'm okay. It's good to see you." *And how is Alec and does he know that I love him?* "How can I help you, Miss Hattie?"

Aunt Hattie gave her a patient smile. "Well, you can start out by telling me why you're stalling out on my Alec."

Marla glanced at Brandy. The girl made a beeline for the back of the building. No help there. So she turned back to Aunt Hattie. "It's a long story."

"Give me the short version, dear."

Marla came around the counter, glad that no one else was waiting out front. "Let's sit a minute."

Hattie Marshall swept into a chair, her silk tunic rustling against her white capris. "He's in love with you."

Marla's stomach churned. Aunt Hattie sure was direct, in spite of being so polite. "I wasn't aware—"

"You don't have to pretend with me," Aunt Hattie continued. "You have to be aware, Marla. I mean, the boy mopes around like one of his puppy dogs. I've never seen Alec like this. He's got it bad and he's hurting."

"I know," Marla said, her throat tightening. She would not break down in front of Alec's aunt. "I know and I care about him but I have Gabby to consider and I'm so afraid I'll fail at everything."

Aunt Hattie waved her hand in the air, her gold and silver bangles moving in a line up her arm. "Honey, if you wait for everything to be perfect, you'll miss all the fun in life. My sister did that, and she died alone and miserable. You have too much life left in you to give up at such a young age."

"Good point." Marla bit her lip. "I hurt him. The truth is, I wanted to go with him to his fancy event but...I chickened out."

Aunt Hattie stood. "I took you to be full of courage. Fearless, I think. I'm not here to change your mind, but I hope you'll reconsider. It's just a couple of hours and he wouldn't have asked you if he didn't want you there with him." Aunt Hattie's gaze moved around the shop and then settled back on Marla. "If you don't do this, you'll wonder for a long time about what might have been. And that's a whole lot of wondering, darlin'."

Marla lifted off the wrought-iron chair. "I understand. Thank you for caring enough to come by."

Aunt Hattie patted Marla's hand. "I want *you* to care enough to consider my words very carefully, Marla. If you change your mind, come by and see me. Believe it or not, I used to be just about your size. I have several formal gowns going to waste in my closet. We'll find one for you." Then she smiled and waltzed over to the counter. "And I'll take an éclair for the road, please."

Friday came and went.

Marla and her staff, along with her mother, got the cupcakes iced and the cookies decorated.

Saturday morning found them all back at the shop doing last-minute things. Her dad even came to help load up the various containers and give her moral support.

Gabby read books and colored pictures in the office, where Marla could see her. Her daughter seemed happier these days, more carefree and trusting.

Marla wanted to feel the same way. Was she sabotaging her own happiness because she was just too afraid to take another chance?

She pushed away her hurt and instead went over the checklist of goodies.

"Bone of Confection."

Brandy pointed to three dozen cream-dressed cupcakes with tiny little doggy bone candies on top.

"In the Doghouse Dutch Chocolate."

"Right here, all three dozen."

"Shelter Me Chiffon Cream."

"Another three dozen."

"Puppy Chow Dark Chocolate."

"Five dozen."

And so it went. They had enough confections to feed the whole town.

Around three in the afternoon, they were finally

done counting and sorting and Marla was ready to load everything into the van and make the delivery—something she dreaded doing.

Busy with directing the assembly line to her van, she felt a tug on her leg. "Mommy?"

"Yes, sweetheart."

"I drew you a picture."

Marla leaned down to take the heavy white piece of paper. "Thanks. How about I look at it later."

Gabby's bottom lip jutted out. "No, right now, Mommy."

"Okay." Marla still held the paper, but she took the time to look at the picture. With a gasp, she fell to her knees in front of Gabby. "Honey, this is so sweet."

The picture showed a little girl and a woman, holding hands. Next to them, there was a dark-haired man holding a puppy.

Gabby bobbed her head. "That's you and me. And that's Mr. Alec and the puppy he's bringing us."

Tears filled Marla's eyes. "I love it," she said. "Maybe one day, you can meet Alec."

Gabby grinned and twirled. "Memaw says he's having a big party tonight. Are you going?"

"No," Marla said, her heart crumbling like a cookie. "I want to stay home with you."

"We could both go," Gabby suggested. "Like Cinderella and Belle, together."

Marla's breath caught in her throat. "Honey, this is going to be a big party with lots of people there. Men and women."

"And little girls in pretty dresses?"

That princess gene always trickled down, Marla thought.

"I don't know if this is a good party for little girls, honey."

Mom came up, her smile full of understanding. "You know what, I think your mom should go to the party and then maybe, just maybe, if you want to go and see her there, Papaw and I can bring you by for just a little while."

"If I get scared, you'd take me home?"

"Yes. If you don't like being there, we'll bring you home. I promise."

Gabby looked up at Marla. "Can I see my puppy if I go?"

Marla's heart did a frantic leap. She stared up at her mother. "Mom...?"

"Honey, she's asking this, not me. I think it's time."

"But all those people?"

"What if we let her meet Alec and the puppy in a private spot?"

Marla stood, tears forming in her eyes. "Mom, I'm so afraid. I don't want her to be hurt ever again."

Mom reached for Marla and whispered in her ear, "And I don't want my little girl to be hurt ever again. But I can't hold you back. Don't hold Gabby back, okay?"

Marla nodded and then she started laughing. "I can't just show up, can I?"

"You are an invited guest," Mom said. "But you do need to start getting ready. You don't have long."

Marla held a hand up. "What about all of this?"

Gabby had been hanging on every word. "I'll help, Mommy."

Dad and Brandy and the whole staff all gathered around. "We'll get everything delivered," he said. "We're all old pros at this stuff."

Brandy nodded, her eyes misty. "You need to call Miss Hattie. Find a dress and I'll meet you back here to get your hair and makeup done."

Mom laughed and tugged at Marla's apron. "And Gabby and I will help get you ready, right?"

Gabby bobbed her head. "In a princess dress."

Dad cleared his throat. "What am I supposed to do?"

Mom took charge. "Order a pizza—and you can drive Cinderella to the ball."

"And I get to come later, right?" Gabby asked, her dark eyes bright with hope.

"Yes," Marla said, her heart sure now. "Yes. I want you to meet Alec tonight and I know you'll like him as much as I do."

"And my puppy, too," Gabby reminded her.

Marla almost backed out. "Mom, have we enticed her too much with the promise of a puppy?"

"We're taking the next step," Mom said. "If she can tolerate Dipsey's Irish banter, this girl can tolerate anything."

Marla prayed that she'd made the right decision. Her future—and Gabby's—depended on it.

Chapter Twenty-One

Alec mingled with his guests, the knot in his tuxedo bow tie straining at his neck. Rory was here, smiling and talking to everyone. Blain was working the crowd both as security and as a guest. No sign of Hunter—but then, Hunter didn't do well in crowds. People kept coming through the door and Alec kept glancing at each of them, hoping beyond hope that one special person would appear.

But he supposed that kind of hope only happened in fairy tales. So he focused on what was taking place tonight.

His dream had finally come true. Soft music played as he greeted the crowds. The team of volunteers Aunt Hattie had corralled to help decorate had outdone themselves. Posters of service dogs with their humans were displayed along the walls and across the big windows, while out in the training yard near the kennels, several owners answered questions and gave demonstrations with their trained dogs. Glittering ribbons in red, white and blue curled and twisted over the posters and a big banner announcing the Alexander and Vivian Caldwell

Service Dog Association Training Facility hung across the balcony leading to the offices upstairs. The tables were decorated with glittery colored papers over the white tablecloths, and bouquets of red and white carnations in blue vases festooned with red bows, sat in the center of each table.

And the food.

Shrimp and crab dip, corn fritters, catfish fingers and a variety of other appetizers filled several of the serving stations. But the one that stood out and had everyone talking was the dessert table.

Marla and her staff had certainly worked hard to capture the fun behind this night. And the purpose.

Alec wanted her here, wanted her to be a part of the celebration. Wanted her with him for the rest of his life. He'd hoped to see her when she delivered everything this afternoon, but when her father and a few helpers had shown up, Alec's heart had sunk. It was over. Her dad's somber expression had proved that. Now the night wore on and with each ticking second that went by, his heart sank.

Marla didn't want him in her life.

He felt a gentle tug on his arm. Aunt Hattie stood with a sweet smile on her ruby-red lips. Wearing a flowing caftan in an off-white color, she looked every bit the society dame.

"Hello, beautiful," Alec said, giving her a hug.

"Hello, yourself," she replied, her eyes sparkling. "I just visited the kennels out back. So many wonderful animals." Her smile held a hint of mischief. "I had hoped to see a puppy or two out there."

"Do you want to adopt a puppy?" he asked, his hand on her arm.

"Oh, no. Angus is quite enough for me. He's my best buddy."

"Mine, too," Alec said. "You're fashionably late. It's about time to do the obligatory announcements and acknowledgements." He pointed to where a podium had been placed near the jazz ensemble. "Care to join me in the spotlight?"

"Oh, no. You go ahead," she said. "I'm waiting for Delton." She craned her neck and waved to people.

Thinking he was too exhausted for his own good, Alec wondered why his aunt was acting so strange tonight. Maybe she was tired, too. She'd been out taking some clothes to "a person in need" earlier.

Alec gave her a quick kiss and then headed to the podium. His assistant alerted the band to wind down the music and Alec stepped up to the waiting mic, his leg wound throbbing a silent protest. After the music ended and the crowd's chatter died down to a soft whisper, he tapped the mic.

"I'm Alec Caldwell," he began. "I'd like to thank you all for coming here tonight to help us raise continued funding for our new service dog training facility." He pointed to the banner hanging on the landing. "I won't repeat that rather long name, but I do want to recognize my parents, Alexander and Vivian Caldwell. I'm blessed to have inherited the fruits of my family's labors and my mother left me precise instructions to do *good* with the Caldwell Foundation. This project is my first attempt to do that. With the opening of this facility, we can not only train service dogs, but we can also place them with deserving humans—and, well, train the humans, too."

Everyone laughed and applauded. He went on to

thank everyone again, to name names of board members and sponsors and to invite everyone out to the kennels to meet some of the animals they'd already been working with.

He finished and cued the band to start back up. Then he turned to find something cool to drink. Relief that he'd made it through that speech made him relax but his heart was still heavy.

Because one person was missing.

He was headed toward the kennels when Annabelle rushed up and hugged him. "Alec, this is the best party ever."

Alec held her at arm's length and took in her heavy mascara and white-blond hair. Annabelle wore a provocative red dress and her ever-present cloying perfume.

"Thanks," he said, carefully extracting himself from her grip. "I'm glad you came."

When the music started back up, he watched as the crowd began to part, thinking everyone wanted to dance. But a woman coming through the crowd caught his eye.

Not just any woman. Marla.

"Alec, dance with me," Annabelle said, her hand reaching for him.

"No, thanks," he said. "Excuse me."

Without looking back, he started toward Marla, his heart so full he thought he might not ever be able to breathe again. She wore a deep blue dress that flared at the waist in layers of some sort of soft flowing material. Her hair shined in a red-gold halo that was caught up against her neck in a twisted chignon. She wore simple pearls on her ears and around her neck.

Alec walked toward her and accepted that he was in love with her. And she was here. She'd come to him.

Marla almost bolted when she saw Alec with that same blonde again. But she told herself to keep walking toward him, not away from him. She had to do this, here, tonight, before she lost her courage. She had to have faith that he wanted her and not the blonde, that Gabby was smarter and stronger than Marla had given her credit for, and that God had a plan in all of their lives.

The dress her mom and Miss Hattie had altered to fit her seemed to lift and float in a cloud of taffeta and chiffon as she moved through the crowded room. The black pumps her mother had loaned her sparkled across the vamps with two matching sapphire clips Brandy secured from a boutique next door to the shop. And she wore her own pearls—a precious gift from her late husband.

I feel like Cinderella, she thought, as her gaze caught Alec's and stayed there. She didn't want this to end at midnight, however. She wanted to be simple, plain Marla who loved handsome, heroic Alec. And she wanted to be a good mother to her little girl and own the best bakery in town.

That was what her fairy tale looked like.

Just full of love, pure and simple. Love with Alec and love filled with God's touch.

Alec met her in the middle of the dance floor as whispers and smiles drifted around them. The music changed tempo and went into a slow, age-old tune. Alec didn't bother asking Marla to dance. He swept her into his arms and started waltzing her around the dance floor.

"Hello," he said against her ear.

"Hi." She smiled up at him. "Sorry I'm late."

"Better late than never," he whispered.

They didn't need any more words, but Marla had so much to say. "Alec—"

"Let's just dance," he said. Then he pulled her close and held his cheek to hers in an old-fashioned way that made her love him even more. Alec Caldwell was a true gentleman.

When the dance ended, they were applauded. Alec grinned and took her by the hand. "I need some air."

"Me, too."

When they were outside, he tugged her toward the noise of barking dogs. "Let me show you the kennel barn."

"Before you do that," she said, "I have a special request."

He stopped, his hand still in hers. "Yes, I'd love to spend the rest of my life loving you."

Marla felt a flutter inside her stomach. "Well, there is that." She smiled up at him. "I'd like to show you how much I love you, too. Forever. But right now I have one very special request."

"Name it."

She didn't want to cry but the tears threatened to spill out of her eyes. "I need a puppy."

Alec stopped, a breath caught in his throat. "You mean—?"

"Gabby wants a puppy," Marla said huskily. "From you."

"Marla, are you sure?"

"No, but Gabby seems sure. She drew a picture of us. Her and me and you with a puppy. She wants to come to the party to meet you, but we might need to keep her away from the crowd."

He glanced around, panic sweeping through him. Alec had never been so scared to meet a little girl. "We can meet in the kennel office. It's big and roomy, with lots of light."

Marla nodded. "Okay. But we need a puppy."

"I don't have any here yet," he said on a note of regret. "I can arrange to get one."

Seeing the disappointment in Marla's eyes, he wished he could have been more prepared. "I don't think any of the bigger dogs would work. They're more aggressive."

"I have a dog."

They both turned to see Hunter Lawson standing there in the shadows, wearing jeans and a plaid shirt.

"Hunter, hello," Alec said, surprised to see his friend.

"Hi." Hunter stalked up and shoved Roxie at Alec. "Just take her, man. I…I think she can help the little girl, like she helped me."

"Are you sure?" Marla asked, tears streaming down her face.

Hunter nodded. "Yep. Preacher keeps telling me I need to let go of some things. But hey—you know how hard that can be." He shrugged. "Anyway, I gotta go away for a while. I can't take Roxie with me and, well, a little bird told me you might know someone who could take her."

Alec held the little poodle and reached out a hand to Hunter. "You don't know what this means."

"Yeah, I kind of do," Hunter said, shaking Alec's hand. He glanced at Marla. "Just take good care of her."

"We will," Marla said. "You…you can visit her anytime."

Hunter didn't speak. He just nodded and backed away, and then he stomped to his motorcycle, cranked it and rode away into the night.

Roxie barked at him and started licking Alec's face.

While Marla stood there and cried.

Marla waited outside the long kennel barn, nerves causing her to close her eyes and take a deep breath. Her parents were on their way here with Gabby.

Dear God, let this be right. Let this sweet little dog help my daughter to heal and to accept Alec. Help us to become a family, Lord.

When she heard a car pull around to the side of the main building, she recognized her daddy's truck. The doors opened and Gabby hopped out, followed by Mom and Dad.

"Look at me, Mommy," Gabby called.

She had on a light blue princess dress, her favorite.

"You look so pretty," Marla said, gathering Gabby close. "Are you ready for this, baby?"

"Uh-huh." Gabby glanced around. "Where's Mr. Alec?"

"He's inside the kennel barn. It's where they keep the dogs."

"I hear them barking."

Gabby reached out a hand to Marla. Marla glanced at her parents.

"Go ahead, honey," Mom said. "We'll be right here if you need us."

Marla took Gabby to the office door, her fears shouting at her to hold back. But that courage Miss Hattie thought she possessed pulled her forward. "You're not scared, are you, Gabby-bug?"

Gabby looked up at her with trusting eyes. "No. Are you scared, Mommy?"

"Not anymore," Marla said.

They walked down the short, lighted hallway and into the office. Alec stood there with little Roxie in his arms. He looked as nervous as Marla felt.

Gabby glanced at Marla and then she stared across at Alec.

"Gabby, this is my friend Alec. And this little dog is Roxie. She's very special and she needs a good friend."

Gabby smiled shyly. "I can be a good friend."

Then Marla watched, tears in her eyes, as her daughter let go of her hand and walked toward the man in the tuxedo who was holding a toy poodle.

Alec shot Marla an amazed glance. "Hi, Gabby," he said, his voice quiet. "This is Roxie. Want to meet her?"

Gabby stopped a couple of feet from him and bobbed her head, her hands clasped against her dress.

Alec bent down and set Roxie on the floor. The little dog ran straight to Gabby. Gabby dropped down with a giggle and let Roxie lick her face. "Look, Mommy. She likes me."

Marla put a hand to her mouth and cried. When she looked up, she saw tears streaming down Alec's face, too. They stood there with the little girl and the little poodle between them.

And watched the unconditional love unfolding right in front of their eyes.

November

Marla went into the den at Caldwell House. "Okay, Thanksgiving meal is on the table. Come and get it."

Her parents and Aunt Hattie, along with her friend Delton, all got up from watching a parade on television and trailed into the formal dining room across the hallway. Gabby and Roxie both came running behind them, with Angus close on their heels. Gabby now had two dogs to make her feel safe.

Alec kissed Marla and laughed. "I like cooking with you. I can't wait until we make this official."

Marla glanced at the diamond on her left ring finger. "Well, the flower girl is definitely ready. And so is the bride."

"So is the favorite aunt," Aunt Hattie said with a chuckle. "A ceremony at the church and the reception right here in the garden. Perfect."

"A Christmas wedding," Alec said while they all settled into their chairs. "Could I be any more blessed?"

"I want more grandchildren," Mom replied with her own grin. "But until then, yes, we're all blessed."

Marla took Alec's hand and held tight while her dad said grace. They *were* all blessed.

Gabby loved little Roxie and she loved Alec now, too. He'd been careful to let Gabby get used to him, but Roxie had been the bond between them. The little dog protected Gabby with a fierceness that rivaled any bigger dog and she'd taken to her official training as if she knew exactly what was expected of her. Marla could only guess that Roxie had lost someone she loved, too.

Alec's scars had been physical, but he had helped

to heal their hidden scars and he'd shown Marla how to love again.

She couldn't wait to be his wife.

But for now, she would enjoy just being in the same room with all the people she loved. Especially Gabby.

And the man she'd met over the remains of a wedding cake.

"What's for dessert?" Dad asked.

"Pumpkin pie and…I'm Crazy About You caramel-apple cupcakes," Alec said with a wink to Marla. "Marla's Marvelous Desserts are in the house."

"Forever," Gabby said, a big drumstick in her hand. "Aunt Hattie says we will love each other forever and ever."

"Amen," Dad replied.

Angus and Roxie both woofed in agreement.

* * * * *

Dear Reader,

This is the first in a series of four books set in the fictional town of Millbrook, Florida. The Men of Millbrook Lake is a series of my heart, and these stories reflect my new home in the Florida Panhandle. Living near water brings me peace and calm, but I've also learned that the storms come when you're living in paradise.

Alec and Marla both have experienced their own storms, but they can see that they are blessed to live in a town where people watch out for each other and love each other. A town where forgiveness is as natural as the changing tides. They both have scars, but Marla saw the beauty in Alec in spite of his injuries, and Alec found the joy in Marla in spite of her grief. When they come together to help her fragile daughter, they begin to heal.

I hope you enjoyed this story and I invite you to look for *Her Holiday Protector*, the next book in this series. It's Blain Kent's story and it's a gritty suspense drama with a theme of justice and doing what's right. I hope my quaint town of Millbrook Lake will uplift you and help you escape from your own storms.

Until next time, may the angels watch over you. Always.

Lenora Worth

REQUEST YOUR FREE BOOKS!

2 FREE INSPIRATIONAL NOVELS
PLUS 2
FREE
MYSTERY GIFTS

LII5

JUST CAN'T GET ENOUGH OF INSPIRATIONAL ROMANCE?

Join our social communities
and talk to us online!
You will have access to the latest
news on upcoming titles and special
promotions, but most important,
you can talk to other fans about your
favorite Love Inspired® reads.

 www.Facebook.com/LoveInspiredBooks

 www.Twitter.com/LoveInspiredBks

Harlequin.com/Community

LISOCIAL